HOLLYWOOD PRINCESS

JENNY OLDFIELD

Illustrated by
Paul Hunt

Hodder
Children's
Books

a division of Hodder Headline

With thanks to Bob, Karen and Katie Foster, and to the staff and guests at Lost Valley Ranch, Deckers, Colorado

First published in Great Britain in 2000
by Hodder Children's Books

A Catalogue record for this book is available from the British Library

ISBN 0 340 75728 0

Typeset by Avon Dataset Ltd, Bidford-on-Avon, Warks

Printed and bound in Great Britain by
The Guernsey Press Co. Ltd, Channel Islands

Hodder Children's Books
a division of Hodder Headline
338 Euston Road
London NW1 3BH

1

'Back off there! Give us some room to unload this horse.' Ben Marsh, the new head wrangler at Half-Moon Ranch, gave orders for Kirstie Scott and her friend, Lisa Goodman, to stand clear.

'C'mon, Lucky, you heard what the man said.' Gently Kirstie dug her heels into the palomino's sides, well behind the cinch strap.

Her good-natured horse hardly needed to be told. He willingly gave way to the horse-trailer that had just pulled up in the yard.

Kirstie saw that Lisa had more of a problem with Jitterbug. The skittish sorrel never liked coming up too close to anything she didn't understand. And big trucks containing something that banged and thudded against the metal sides came well within that category. Back went her ears, flat against her head. Then she swung her rear end round and kicked out.

'Whoa!' In the short struggle to get Jitterbug back in order, Lisa lost her baseball cap. But she tightened the reins and soon won the battle. Within a few seconds she'd joined Kirstie by the fence of the round-pen, and together they watched the arrival of the new horse.

'OK, Charlie, you can let down the ramp.' Keeping a wary eye on a group of onlookers gathering outside the ranch house, Ben carried on handing out the orders. Two weeks in to the spring season on the dude ranch, he was still prickly and abrupt with the junior wrangler.

('Give him time,' Kirstie's mother, Sandy, told her when Ben's name had come up at supper one evening. 'It can't be easy for him to settle into a new job with Hadley breathing down his neck.')

Kirstie understood what she meant. Glancing round now, she spotted the cantankerous old man casting a critical eye on proceedings. Until last fall, when he'd retired as head wrangler, unloading a new horse would've been Hadley's task.

'Bad idea to do it just as the trail-rides get back to base,' he muttered to Kirstie when he caught her eye. 'Too many folks around.'

'I guess it can't be helped.' She watched Ben put a foot on to the lowered ramp. Inside the box, the new arrival squealed and snorted.

'Where's this horse come from?' Lisa asked, dusting down her cap and jamming it on top of her unruly red hair.

Kirstie shrugged. She was tired after a day leading an intermediate group of riders on Coyote Trail. 'Don't know too much about her. The plates on the truck say Wyoming.'

'How old is she?' Keeping Jitterbug on a tight

rein, Lisa craned forward for a better view.

'Don't know.'

'Name?'

'Dunno.'

'What colour?'

Kirstie replied this time with a big, silent shrug.

'Gee, you're really on the ball on this one!' Lisa grinned at her.

Kirstie smiled back. 'Yeah. Ask Hadley.'

'Hadley?' Lisa turned her dazzling smile on the ex-wrangler.

'Huh?' He watched with narrowed eyes from under the wide brim of his tall white stetson as Ben Marsh disappeared inside the truck.

'What do you know about this new horse?'

A small shrug from Hadley. 'Ask Ben.'

So Lisa had to put a brake on her curiosity.

The head wrangler was obviously caught up right then, busy untying the horse after her long journey and leading her towards the ramp.

Sitting in the saddle in the late afternoon sun, Kirstie felt her curiosity rising. This was a high-spirited mare, to judge by the amount of noise she was still making. Sure, she knew they needed an extra mount to join the string of horses who daily trod the trails at Half-Moon Ranch. Business was good, according to her brother, Matt.

Hadley had moved out of the bunkhouse and taken up residence in Brown Bear Cabin a little way up the hill. The Scotts had also built four new cabins for guests nearby. This meant that the ramuda was having to expand too to cope with more visitors. They already had Chigger and Squeaky settled in with the herd in Red Fox Meadow; one a black and white paint, one a bay gelding. Now the mare from Wyoming was to join them.

But ideally the horse would be quiet and well mannered, the type any rider could handle, and this mare sure didn't fit *that* description.

'Wow!' A kid in the crowd by the house got first sight of the mare.

All the guests stepped forward for a better view.

'Back off!' Charlie warned, stretching his arms wide and walking towards them.

The new arrival stamped and kicked inside the box.

'She's a real beaut!' one guy said. Dusty after their day in the saddle, still the dude riders hung around instead of going up to their cabins to shower and get ready for supper.

'C'mon, Ben!' Lisa was growing impatient alongside Jitterbug, who danced and pranced by the fence.

The unseen horse seemed to be quietening down. There was less kicking and stamping, more manoeuvring into position. Then a heavy clunk of hooves as she took a step towards the ramp.

'Oh my!' a woman visitor added to the admiring gasps. 'What wouldn't you give to ride a horse like that!'

'C'mon!' Lisa risked taking Jitterbug a couple of paces across the yard. Then she saw what everyone was sighing over. 'Kirstie, won't you look at this!'

The horse had appeared on the ramp at last and Kirstie could see that she was one in a million.

For a start, there was her colour. Pure white from head to toe. Not cream or grey; pure, dazzling white.

Then there was her long, silky mane falling forward over the prettiest face. Dark, dark, expressive eyes and a dished nose like an Arab; head up, neck arched.

'Ohh!' Kirstie joined in with the adoring crowd.

Ben kept the lead-rope short and walked the horse into full view.

She stepped high and dainty on long, straight legs. Her body was sleek and muscular, without an ounce of extra weight.

'Hey, Miss Glamour-puss!' Slowly Lisa inched forward on Jitterbug.

Still strung-out and nervous of her new surroundings, the horse pulled at her rope. She dipped back on her haunches, ready to raise her front feet and rear up. But Ben held tight and led her out of the sun into the long shadow of the house.

'Easy!' The wrangler spoke soothingly and handled her well. 'Charlie, open the corral gate,' he ordered, giving the horse time to settle.

She turned her head this way and that, sniffed the air, listened to the other horses in the meadow.

And Kirstie had time to drink in the appearance of the new arrival. 'American Albino!' she whispered to Lisa. 'Classic mixture of Arab and Morgan horse, started off in Nebraska. The Lone Ranger rode a horse like that in all the old movies.'

'Don't give me that!' her friend breathed back. 'All I know is, she's beautiful!'

Kirstie had to agree. And she noticed now that the mare didn't seem fazed by the situation, that in fact she might just be playing to the crowd. The way her head was up made her look cocky and self-assured, and her walk as Ben led her towards the corral was more of a prancing strut. Yeah, she was definitely showing off!

'The horse has star quality!' Lisa insisted.

She pranced and danced, she jaunted and skipped. Her eyes darted from the crowd by the house to Lisa on Jitterbug and Kirstie on Lucky.

Dismissing the opposition of the sorrel mare, she came up sideways towards the handsome palomino. Look at me! she said with the carriage of her head and tail and her high-stepping walk.

'Hey, she's flirting with him!' Lisa laughed out loud.

Ben wrestled with the lead-rope to bring the white mare back into line. 'Walk on!' he ordered, clicking his tongue and leaning with his shoulder against her withers.

Still grinning, Lisa called out after him. 'She's a drop-dead gorgeous horse! What's her name?'

The wrangler led the mare on, answering over her shoulder as she swept by. 'Hollywood Princess.'

'That's a great name!' Lisa sighed.

'Yeah,' Kirstie agreed. 'She could be in the movies!'

And she knew that a new star had been born at Half-Moon Ranch.

'Hollywood does tricks,' Ben told Lisa after the group of guests had wandered off to their cabins.

Lisa and Kirstie were unsaddling their own horses in the corral. By now, the shadow of Eagle's Peak had swept down the valley, bringing cool air, fading the red roof of the barn to dull brown and turning the stands of aspens and ponderosa pines into tall, dark sentinels standing guard over the ranch.

Lisa slung Jitterbug's saddle over a hook in the tack-room and came to stand on the porch. 'What kind of tricks?'

'Watch.' Ben left off brushing the Albino. He came round to her head, stood face to face about a yard from her, then offered her the palm of his right hand. 'Put it there, partner!'

Hollywood considered the command. Should she or shouldn't she obey? When she saw that she had Lisa, Kirstie and Hadley hovering in the background as an audience, she decided to cooperate. Gracefully she bent her right knee and raised her foot to the level of Ben's outstretched hand. She rested her hoof gently in his palm and let him shake it up and down.

'Cool!' Lisa laughed, then clapped. 'What else can she do?'

'Waste of time,' Hadley grumbled quietly, but loud enough for Kirstie to hear. 'Darn fool tricks don't impress no one!'

'I think you're wrong about that!' Kirstie murmured back, watching her friend's wide-eyed, admiring stare.

'C'mon, Hollywood, give me a kiss!' Ben stuck out his head and turned his cheek towards the horse's lips.

Playing hard to get, the mare shook her head.

'Aw, c'mon!' Ben pleaded.

Hollywood snorted, relaxed her lips and nuzzled up to Ben's cheek.

'Yeah, good girl!' The wrangler popped a mint from his jeans pocket into the horse's mouth. 'That's not all,' he told Lisa. 'She can count to four.'

'No way!'

'Sure she can. And you can make her rear up on her hind legs with you on her back, just by the touch of your heels.' Ben picked up the brush

11

and finished grooming his protégée.

'Like the Lone Ranger!' Lisa gave Kirstie a short, what-gives-with-you glance. 'Hey, Hadley, did you ever see a horse as smart as this?'

The old man sniffed and shrugged. 'That horse should be out in the ramuda by now,' he grunted, tipping his hat forward and turning up his collar as he walked off.

Kirstie saw Ben pause in mid brush-stroke. Though his face was in the shadow of the tall barn, she could still detect a flicker of annoyance. But he decided to let it pass. 'Sure thing,' he agreed, untethering Hollywood from the post and getting set to lead her to the meadow. 'You girls coming along to see how she settles in?'

2

'How come she performs those tricks for you?'
As they walked together over the footbridge
across Five Mile Creek towards Red Fox Meadow,
Lisa wanted to know the horse's background.

'Because I taught her,' came the reply.

'Huh?'

For Kirstie, it was like being a fly-on-the-wall,
listening, looking. No need to say anything, since
Lisa did all the talking. Sometimes her friend's

gossipy style got her down. Sometimes, like now, Kirstie found it useful. She looked up at a huge, pale moon rising in the twilit sky and tuned in to Ben's answer.

'Hollywood worked on the same ranch as me out in Wyoming,' he explained. 'A ranch by the name of Echo Basin, out near Rock Springs. It's a working cattle ranch, and Hollywood here was one of the best cutting horses around.'

Kirstie noticed that the mare seemed to know she was being talked about. She gave her little 'Look at me!' skip and prance, shaking her silky mane and arching her neck.

'Hmm. A working ranch horse! And here was me thinking she was nothing but a glamour-puss.' Lisa was growing more fascinated by the second.

'No way.' Ben let Kirstie walk ahead to open the gate to the meadow. 'This little lady is tough as they come. She's an ex-champion as a matter of fact.'

'And you trained her to do those cute tricks?'

'Me and a couple of the other guys.' The wrangler stroked the horse's neck and steadied her as they waited. 'When I heard she was up for sale, the week after I left to come down here, I told the boss right away . . .'

Ben's voice faded as Kirstie stepped through the long grass and swung the gate open. She watched the herd gather at the far side of the meadow, picked out Lucky's pale mane and tail and wondered why he didn't come galloping to meet her.

Too busy working out the stranger arrived in their midst, she guessed. And maybe the tiniest bit jealous of all the attention Hollywood Princess was getting. Horses could sulk too, as she very well knew.

'So Sandy took my word for it that this here is the smartest type of horse.' Ben went on singing the newcomer's praises. 'Sure, she hasn't done trail-riding before, but she's a real quick learner.'

'And so-oo beautiful!' Lisa breathed, delighted when Ben handed her the lead-rope and allowed her to take the horse into the meadow.

Puh-lease! Kirstie thought. In her opinion, this was a little OTT.

Ben folded his arms and watched the horse through the gate.

Hollywood's ears were pricked forward, focused on the herd. Her white coat seemed to reflect the moonlight, and while everything else was drained of colour, she alone stood out. She went forward boldly, her feet brushing through the grass, the lines of her strong body clean and sharp.

Kirstie saw Jitterbug cut away from the herd and move towards them, meaning perhaps to challenge the new mare and put her in her place. The sorrel's head was up; she flicked her tail as she loped across the field, hooves thumping into the firm ground.

'Huh!' Kirstie turned to Hollywood to watch her reaction and gave a grunt of surprise.

This was a transformed horse they were looking at. Down went the show-off's head into a humble, please-be-nice-to-me posture. It caught Jitterbug off guard, so that she stopped suddenly and took in the new message.

Hollywood's head was still down and her jaw

was working in a chewing motion. *'Don't hurt me!'* it pleaded. *'I'm only a poor, defenceless, homeless creature!'*

It worked. Jitterbug circled slowly, allowing the other horses to join her. Together they decided that the white mare was no threat to their group.

'Hah!' Kirstie grunted as Johnny Mohawk, one of the best-looking stallions at Half-Moon Ranch, took over from Jitterbug and stepped forward. He came right up close to Hollywood and nudged his nose against hers, reassuring, welcoming.

She nudged back, slowly letting her head come up into its proud arch, giving Johnny the wide-eyed, innocent look.

He was smitten. From now on he would look out for the beautiful newcomer, protecting her from the other mares' jealousy, canoodling with her in corners whenever he got the chance.

'Easy!' Lisa cried, calling Kirstie out of the meadow and closing the gate on the horses.

'Smart!' Kirstie conceded. Calculating and clever, but not the type of horse that got through to her.

'No problem.' Satisfied that Hollywood Princess would settle into the ramuda, Ben led the way back to the creek.

They stopped once, on the footbridge, to look back and check.

And it was as if Hollywood was saying, '*One more twirl before you go!*'

Because she reared up high on her hind legs. Caught sideways on, her front feet pawed the night air, her long mane fell back from her face and neck and flew in the breeze. Classic movie-star pose, and truly, truly beautiful.

'Now, sir, have you done a lot of riding before you came to Half-Moon Ranch?' Ben asked. He was carrying out the head wrangler's most important task of the week, which was to allocate a suitable horse to each dude rider.

'Some, I guess.' The guy at the head of the line shuffled forward a step or two.

Ben looked him up and down, saw that he was heavy and out of condition. 'I'd say Crazy Horse would be good for you.' Asking the rider his name and chalking it up on the board in the box marked Crazy Horse, he asked Charlie to find the guy a saddle and fix him up with the placid light sorrel mount.

Kirstie leaned on the fence next to Hadley, waiting for the new batch of trail-riders to get ready.

Next in line was a fifteen-year-old girl with a brash smile, brand new cowboy boots and leather chaps.

'You ridden on a round-up before?' Ben asked.

'Sure. Hundreds of times.' The girl sniffed and screwed up her small mouth between her clipped sentences.

Ben studied her closely. 'I'm talking cattle round-up here.'

'Yeah!' The girl's attempt to meet the wrangler's gaze failed. She dropped her head and scuffed the toes of her boots in the yellow dust.

'Hundreds?'

'A few.'

'How many?'

'One. I was here last spring,' the girl admitted.

'Hey, all right! And which horse did you ride last year, Martina?' Ben checked a list from his pocket. 'Couldn't have been Yukon, could it?'

Sheepishly, the city girl nodded.

'Well, take her again this year. Yukon's a great little horse, a paint. Paints are my favourites.' Cheerfully Ben chalked the girl's name in Yukon's box.

'I reckon he handled that OK,' Kirstie murmured. Without meaning to, she was still giving Ben Marsh marks out of ten for everything he did.

Hadley as usual said nothing. He just looked.

'OK, Ma'am, let's find you a nice horse.' Ben was already dealing with the next woman in the line, who was tall and slim and looking a million dollars in designer jeans and tailored cowboy shirt.

'You know the one I'd like!' she said to the wrangler with a sugar-sweet smile.

'Yuck!' Lisa had crept up on Kirstie from behind.

'Miaow!' Kirstie hissed back at her.

'Me?' Lisa opened her green eyes wide.

'I'd like to ride that wonderful white horse that arrived yesterday!' the woman cooed.

'Well now . . .' Ben took a step back and frowned. 'Can you just give me your name, Ma'am, so I can check you off my list?'

'Mitzy Donohoe. Hollywood Princess is the best of the bunch,' the woman hurried on. She had a slow, southern voice and a wheedling tone. Also, a way of keeping very close to the person she was speaking to, Kirstie noted.

'Well, Mitzy, Hollywood ain't settled in yet. So I'd feel a whole lot happier putting you on . . . let's see now . . . Cadillac!' Ben led her across the corral, through a throng of saddled horses waiting for their riders.

'Nice one!' Lisa whispered.

Cadillac was Matt Scott's horse, a good-looking creamy coloured gelding with an aristocratic air. When Mitzy met him, she nodded and smiled.

'Ben's OK,' Lisa commented.

Kirstie nodded. Hadley didn't.

'Pity he's not . . .' Lisa paused, pursing her lips and tipping her head to one side.

'Not what?' Kirstie gave her a curious look.

'Well, you know . . . pity he's not more . . .'

'Handsome?' Kirstie guessed. Ben's rangy, slightly stooped and shy appearance obviously wasn't to her friend's taste. Studying his short, light brown hair and thin face, she shook her head. 'No, I think that's good.'

'Huh?' Lisa swung her legs over the fence and perched easily.

'You already had enough excitement for one weekend,' Kirstie teased.

'Meaning?'

'Meaning, you went totally OTT over Hollywood yesterday.' Kirstie's grey eyes sparkled with laughter as she pretended to concentrate on the next person in line. 'So if the new wrangler turned out to be anywhere near as gorgeous as the new horse, I reckon you'd never be able to take it!'

'Actually, I think Ben is pretty neat!' Kirstie didn't

let the game drop, even after the guests had all ridden off with Sandy, Ben, Matt and Charlie.

She and Lisa cleared the yard with giant rakes and shovels, making all neat and clean for when the riders returned for lunch.

'You do?' Lisa stopped work to raise an eyebrow.

'Nope. Just kidding.' She looked up to see Hadley leading none other than Hollywood Princess from the barn into the corral, all tacked up and ready to go.

'Your mom asked us to try her out while they were gone,' he explained.

'Great!' Flinging down her rake, Lisa ran eagerly across.

Shying away at the sudden movement, Hollywood pulled hard on the lead-rope.

'Take it easy,' Hadley advised. 'She still spooks at the least little thing.'

'Sorry.' A more subdued Lisa hung back until the horse had settled.

'That's OK. You want to try riding her?' The old wrangler persuaded the nervous horse back into line.

Lisa nodded, then turned to Kirstie. 'How about you first?'

'No, you go ahead,' Kirstie grinned back. No way would she take this moment away from her excited friend.

So Hadley held Hollywood steady while Lisa mounted. Kirstie watched the white mare give a little twitch at the sudden weight of her rider, then stand square and steady. Her ears flicked round to focus on Lisa, who settled in the saddle and gave her a small dig in the ribs. 'Walk on nice and easy,' she said as Hadley let go of the reins.

Smoothly, daintily Hollywood stepped out across the corral. Her gait was even, her action level.

'How does it feel?' Kirstie called as Lisa reined Hollywood to the right.

'Did I die and go to heaven?' Another kick and click of the tongue from Lisa sent Hollywood into a neat trot.

Kirstie turned to Hadley. 'What do you think?'

The old man cast a critical eye. 'Showy,' he grunted.

'Yeah, we know that already. But . . . ?' She waited for more.

'But sound,' he admitted.

Kirstie watched Lisa guide Hollywood out of the corral on to the start of Eden Lake Trail. Ahead lay two hundred yards of smooth, level grass. The white mare's head was up, sensing action. 'Only "sound"?' she prompted.

Lisa dug her heels into Hollywood's flanks, sat deep in the saddle and let her lope. The horse's stride lengthened, her feet pounded in double, rhythmical beats. Loping swiftly, she ate up the ground.

'Yee-hah!' Lisa gave Hollywood her head.

'*Look at me!*' The movie star in Hollywood came out as she broke into a gallop. '*You thought I was just a pretty face. Well, take a look at this burst of speed!*'

It took Kirstie's breath away just to watch.

'That's one classy quarter horse!' Hadley grunted, turning away.

'Where are you going?' Kirstie demanded, torn between staying to watch Hollywood and following Hadley towards the barn.

'To saddle up Chigger and Lucky,' he told her without breaking his stride.

She followed. 'Why? Are we going somewhere?' Behind them, Hollywood's hooves drummed back down the trail.

'Lazy B Ranch.' With a matter-of-fact shove, Hadley went through the barn door and lifted a saddle which sat astride a bale of hay.

Kirstie took the saddle and went to find Lucky in a nearby stall. Outside in the corral, Hollywood and Lisa had just arrived. The mare neighed loudly to let them know she was there. 'What's all this for?' she wanted to know. Getting answers out of Hadley was like squeezing blood from a stone.

'Jim Mullins called. He wants some help on the round-up.'

Kirstie caught her breath as she laid the saddle across Lucky's broad, golden back. 'You, me and Lisa?' she checked.

'Yeah, with Chigger, Lucky and Hollywood,' he added, leading the tacked-up paint out of the barn. 'They're the guys who're gonna do all the work.'

3

Lazy B lay in the valley next to Half-Moon Ranch. Like Kirstie's home, it was hemmed in by steep, wooded mountain slopes which broke on to the skyline as bald, pink granite cliffs. The grazing along the valley bottom, alongside Eden Creek, consisted of a series of green pastures strung out like beads on a necklace and linked by the silver thread of bright water.

It was here that rancher Jim Mullins hoped to

drive and corral his cattle at the end of the spring round-up.

'Easy now, Starlight, don't crowd the cows!' Jim had noticed the arrival of Hadley, Kirstie and Lisa on the brow of Miners' Ridge, but he carried on herding a bunch of eight or ten brown Herefords into a corral by the creek. He and two other cowboys drove the cattle out of a stand of young willows and funnelled them through a natural gulley into a pasture bounded by a razor-wire fence.

Kirstie eased Lucky down the hill, picking their way between pine trees, eagerly noting the dust clouds kicked up by the lowing cattle. Though dirty and hard, this was the kind of work both she and her horse enjoyed.

'Yip, yip!' Jim's call chivvied the last young bullock out of the awkward willow bushes into the meadow. The youngster sank to his hocks in wet mud on the bank of the stream, heaved himself free, then trotted quickly after the rest of the bunch.

'Two units in the culvert to our left!' Hadley

spotted a couple of strays and called quietly to the girls.

Lisa and Hollywood were in the best position to see the cows, so she immediately cut her horse off down the narrow ravine.

'I'll go up on to the ridge.' Kirstie decided that there was a way down into the culvert and that she and Lucky could work the cattle from behind.

Meanwhile, Hadley followed Lisa.

'Easy now, Lucky!' Kirstie kept her voice low and soothing as the palomino's hooves showered grit down into the gulley. The two cows looked up and bellowed. She and Lucky picked their way up the steep slope, over fallen trees and under low, overhanging branches. By the time she reached the top and looked down into the ravine, she saw that the other two riders had already cornered the wary cattle.

'We'll keep them nice and tight together while you come down and drive them forward!' Hadley yelled.

Nodding, Kirstie urged Lucky on down a narrow, dusty track. Two-toed hoof marks showed that the track had been worn by wandering cattle, which meant that there was a chance that the two trapped heifers would see the route as a way out of a tight spot. She wanted to beat them to it by getting Lucky down there as fast as possible.

'Whoa!' Lisa steadied Hollywood as grit and dirt showered down.

The white mare snorted and stamped impatiently, pulling at the bit to show that she wanted to get to work.

'OK!' Kirstie called when she'd finally manoeuvred Lucky into position. She felt the adrenaline pumping through her veins after the steep descent, and the heat coming off her horse. Lucky's shoulders and sides were dark with sweat.

'Lisa, take Hollywood back a couple of steps, and Kirstie, begin to drive them out!' Hadley, the expert, took charge.

Kirstie yipped and waved her arms at the cows, who tossed their heavy heads and turned clumsily in the narrow gap. They blundered through bushes, towards Lisa and Hollywood, who stood firm and forced them out towards Hadley and Chigger.

'Keep 'em moving!' he warned. 'Don't let them double back!'

Lisa and Kirstie yelled and yipped in chorus.

In no time, the cows broke out of the neck of the culvert on to the open slope.

'OK, now cut 'em off down the hill!' Weaving through the trees, making good progress, Hadley issued steady instructions.

The lead cow of the pair trampled through the undergrowth, happy to be driven. But towards the bottom of the slope, the second seemed to have other ideas. She made a sudden break to the left, barging up against Lisa and Hollywood then charging for the freedom of Eden Creek.

'Hey!' Lisa gave a sharp cry and kicked her horse into action. From a sedate walk down the slope, Hollywood gave a supercharged leap. She sprang forward straight into a gallop, mane flowing, head stretched out and streamlined with the rest of her agile body.

Within seconds, the sleek cutting horse had

caught up with the clumsy brown heifer, overtaken her and started to head her back on to the desired track.

'Wow!' Kirstie had been impressed by the sudden burst of speed and the horse's confidence around cattle. It seemed Ben had been right: this was one champion cutter.

Hadley's eyes were narrowed to slits, his jaw clenched tight as he watched the skilful fetch. 'Hmm,' he grunted.

Kirstie grinned and carried on driving the strays towards the meadow. She knew that from the ex head wrangler, a curt little 'Hmm' was praise indeed.

'Nice horse.' Jim commented on Hollywood Princess as the small group of horses, riders and cows plodded into the meadow.

Starlight, his sturdy black mount, seemed to agree. The sixteen-hands-high gelding nudged up close to the Albino for a friendly greeting.

'Ben Marsh convinced Kirstie's mom to bring her over from Echo Basin.' Lisa bubbled with pride on Hollywood's behalf.

'That the new guy?' Turning to Hadley, Jim entered a serious discussion about the merits of the young head wrangler. Together they headed for coffee and a mid-morning break at the ranch house.

Lisa and Kirstie fell behind, in amongst the hard-working wranglers from the Lazy B. As Kirstie was by now learning to expect, the men quickly bunched round the mare.

'Nice smooth action.'

'Look how she slides her hind feet along under her.'

'Great head, clear eye.'

The compliments from these hardened ranch hands flowed as they reached the yard fenced around with rough planks of pine.

Hollywood's head was high, her expression a touch smug, Kirstie thought, as though admiring comments were no more than she deserved.

And when Lisa told the men that the horse did tricks, they clamoured to be shown the full repertoire.

Kirstie saw Lisa grin and swing out of the saddle. She watched Hollywood do the shake-hands routine, then plant a loud kiss on her friend's cheeks.

The Lazy B guys laughed and clapped. 'Can she rear up like Silver?' one asked.

'Like in the movies?' Lisa hesitated and glanced at Kirstie.

Don't even think about it! Kirstie returned a silent, meaningful glare. She was certain that her town-based friend had never tried such a thing in her life.

'Sure she can!' Lisa boasted as she stepped back up into the saddle. 'I just have to give her a little touch with my heels well back from the cinch strap . . .'

Hollywood didn't rear up, but instead backed quickly across the yard.

'Sit down hard in the saddle at the same time as kicking,' a young wrangler suggested.

Lisa frowned and tried his advice.

Still confused, the horse squatted on her haunches, but didn't lift her front feet.

'Lean way back!' someone else shouted. 'Then as she rears you gotta shoot your weight forward to stay in the saddle!'

'Got it!' Lisa tried again.

This time, the message came through loud and clear, and Hollywood threw her head back, raising her front end and tipping Lisa back at an angle of forty-five degrees.

Lisa whipped back, then forward. She had to cling to the saddle horn as the horse reared up.

'Yeah!' The men cheered.

But Kirstie held her breath for five, six seconds as the white horse pranced on two feet. She half-closed her eyes, expecting any second that her friend would give way to gravity and slip over the back rim of the saddle, on to the mare's backside, then drop to the ground beneath those dangerous dancing hooves.

'Nice job, Lisa!' The guys from the ranch appreciated the performance. They were still clapping when Jim and Hadley broke up the show and told everyone that there was a mug of coffee waiting for them in the tack-room.

'Did you see that?' Breathless, her eyes wide with exhilaration, Lisa dismounted and tethered Hollywood alongside Lucky.

'Yeah, but don't go trying that again,' Kirstie muttered. Her heart had been in her mouth as Hollywood had reared.

The comment brought Lisa up short. 'What's your problem, Kirstie?'

'I don't have a problem. I'm just asking you to take it easy on Hollywood, OK?'

Lisa sighed and frowned. 'This couldn't be because we stole your limelight, by any chance?'

'What limelight? What are you talking about?' By this time, she and Lisa were facing each other, hands on hips, their voices raised.

'The attention that you and your precious palomino usually get has come our way all of a sudden. That's what your problem really is. It's nothing to do with that trick being dangerous.'

'You gotta be joking!' Kirstie turned her head to one side and gave a hollow laugh. Deep down, she was afraid that Lisa was about ten per cent correct. But ninety per cent wrong. She turned back to face her. 'Listen, Lisa, this is serious. A horse only does what we ask him to do because he *wants* to cooperate. He's stronger and bigger than us. There's no earthly reason why he should put up with it except for some unknown reason he likes to please.'

'So?' Doubt flickered into Lisa's green eyes.

'So, don't push Hollywood too far . . . that's all I'm saying.' Kirstie had seen a horse turn on a rider who had been too rough or too inexperienced. She knew that a hoof could break bones, that the full weight of a horse could crush a person to death.

A frown gathered between Lisa's brows. She swallowed, and when she spoke, her voice was quiet and subdued. 'OK. Sorry I yelled.'

'Me too.'

Lisa's troubled face brightened. 'So we're OK, you and me?'

Kirstie smiled back. 'C'mon, let's go get some coffee!'

During Monday, Tuesday and Wednesday,

Hollywood Princess's fame spread beyond Half-Moon Ranch and Lazy B to San Luis, Renegade and Marlowe County.

When Charlie Miller drove into Renegade to buy feed for the horses, he was stopped in the street by shopkeepers who had heard all about the new addition to Sandy Scott's ramuda. And when Matt did his usual midweek trip down from vet school in Denver, and he stopped off at San Luis to pick up Kirstie at the end of the school day, he'd already been accosted twice in the cattle-town of Marlowe County by cowboys wanting to know more about the famous white horse.

'Why all the razzmatazz about Hollywood?' Matt asked Kirstie as she slung her bag on to the back seat of his car and slumped into the passenger seat. He told her that the new horse's reputation had spread far and wide.

'Oh gee, don't ask me!' She'd had to spend three whole days listening to Lisa's tales about the magical horse.

'. . . She can count to four!' Lisa had told the entire class.

'That's more than Noah Newman can do!' someone had joked about a kid who had just flunked a math test.

'. . . She's so smart!' Lisa had sighed to a bunch of girls over a lunch break. 'And real pretty, with a long, pure white silky mane!'

'She's the Barbie doll of the horse world!' a cynic had teased. 'The My Little Pony of Half-Moon Ranch!'

'Would you quit talking about Hollywood?' Kirstie had begged Lisa earlier that day. 'Don't you know you're making her out to be more than she is?'

Lisa had given her the widest of her wide-eyed stares. 'Is this Kirstie Scott saying this? Aren't you the one who likes horses better than people?'

'Yeah, but . . .' How could Kirstie say that this hero-worship of Hollywood was making her uneasy?

In any case, Lisa had taken not the least bit of notice.

'. . . You should see her cut a cow out of a culvert and drive her down to the meadow!' She'd gone on to bore yet another bunch of listeners. 'She has this most amazing burst of speed; you've never seen anything like it!'

'If you must know, I think Lisa is obsessed over this horse,' Kirstie told Matt now. 'She keeps telling guys about her "Lone Ranger trick" and making out like Hollywood is the neatest thing since sliced bread.'

Matt glanced at Kirstie and eased the car out from the sidewalk, past the big yellow school bus. 'And what do you think?' he asked quietly.

'I think the same as Hadley.' She recalled the old wrangler's less than enthusiastic verdict after he'd watched the Lone Ranger trick from afar.

They'd all been filing into Jim Mullins's tack-room to get coffee, when Hadley had passed his comment.

'Which was . . . ?' Matt prompted.

Kirstie stared out of the car window at the red-haired figure of her best friend standing chatting at the school gate. Lisa was gossiping hard, grabbing another girl's arm, giving a little squeal and laughing. Typical!

42

'. . . That a horse like Hollywood belongs in a circus, not on a ranch,' she murmured, as Matt drove down the Main Street out of town.

4

'Did you hear the news?' Mitzy Donohoe, the well dressed guest from Philadelphia, rushed up to Matt's car as it drew into the yard at Half-Moon Ranch.

'Good or bad?' Matt got out of the car in his usual unhurried way.

Kirstie too knew not to take the woman too seriously. Every day since she'd arrived, there'd been some new drama to do with lost sunglasses or getting her shirt wet in a rain shower while her group was out on the trail.

'Oh, really terrible news!' Mitzy gasped. 'It's about Hollywood Princess!'

The name made Kirstie stop and turn. She glanced across the yard to the round-pen, where a small knot of people, including her mom and Ben, stood deep in discussion.

Her first thought was that Hollywood must be sick.

'They're going to sell her!' the distressed guest cried. 'Matt, she's a wonderful horse. You have to stop them!'

'That's the first I heard,' he muttered, changing course and heading with Kirstie across the yard.

Mitzy Donohoe kept up a bleating commentary as she followed in their wake. 'That's Jim Mullins. He came from Lazy B expressly to put in an offer for Hollywood; says she's the best ranch horse he's set eyes on for years!'

Kirstie could see that the Jim Mullins part of this was true. She picked out their neighbour's broad frame and balding head, heard his low, even tone as they drew near.

'I'm making you a good offer here, Sandy,' he was saying. 'I'm willing to pay well above the guidelines writ down by breeders in the American White Horse Club.'

Kirstie's mom nodded thoughtfully. She smiled briefly at Matt and Kirstie. 'I hear you, Jim. But the thing is, I ain't thought about selling Hollywood yet awhile.'

The rancher obviously read her hesitation as a hard bargaining tactic. He hitched up his wide leather belt and put more pressure on in return. 'Look at it my way. I run a working ranch, three hundred and sixty-five days a year, twenty-four hours a day. I need the best roping and cutting horses I can find.'

'I know that—'

Jim put up a broad hand to ward off the interruption. 'Hear me out. The horses here at Half-Moon are pleasure horses, right?'

Slowly Sandy nodded.

'You need steady mounts, the kind that don't

mind staying in line and taking their time over things.'

Kirstie listened and frowned. She didn't like the picture he was painting. Cadillac, Silver Flash, Rodeo Rocky . . . Lucky: none of these horses fell into the plodding class.

'Now, with the money I'm willing to pay you for the one horse, you can buy three more plain ordinary quarter horses of the kind you need.' Jim presented the arithmetic with stunning clarity. His expression and posture both said, 'You know it makes sense!'

'Maybe.' Sandy was checking with Matt for his reaction.

'We never turn our backs on a chance to make a few bucks,' Matt said, businesslike as ever.

'Oh!' Behind their backs, Mitzy Donohoe gave a horrified cry.

'Mrs Scott, I don't reckon this is such a good idea . . .' Having kept quiet until now, Ben chipped in with a polite protest.

'Tell you what . . .' Sandy began, ignoring Mitzy and Ben, then breaking off to mutter a few words to Charlie. The ranch hand nodded and ran off to the corral. 'Charlie's been riding Hollywood this afternoon, easing her in on a half-day ride. So she's still tacked up, saddle and all. The least we can do, while we consider your offer, Jim, is to put the horse through her paces for you to have a look at.'

'Good thinking.' The rancher's satisfied nod showed that he judged that things were going his way.

'Kirstie will ride her for you, won't you, honey?'

'Sure.' She sounded relaxed, but it was with mixed feelings that she made for the corral to mount Hollywood. A little bit of her agreed with Matt: if there was money to be made out of the sale, why turn it down? After all, the white horse had only been at Half-Moon Ranch for five days, hardly time to settle down and become part of the place.

On the other hand, it did feel as if they were treating her like a simple commodity, an object to be bartered over and sold for profit. This didn't seem fair to the beautiful creature. And besides, if they sold her to Jim Mullins, what on earth would Kirstie say to Lisa?

'Don't look at me!' Charlie protested, standing in the corral with Hollywood, ready to give Kirstie a leg up. He came somewhere in between Matt and Kirstie's point of view: practical and efficient in his work, but soft-hearted too. 'I don't know any answers!'

Up in the saddle, Kirstie shrugged. This, she realised, was the first time she'd actually ridden the graceful new horse.

And, wow, did Hollywood flow as she stepped out of the corral! Her gait was light and smooth; it was like floating on air.

'Take her along by the creek!' Sandy called, raising her hand to shield her eyes from the low sun.

So Kirstie reined Hollywood in a wide curve, keeping her this side of Five Mile Creek and turning her towards an open stretch of land running as far as the start of Eden Lake Trail. About halfway down, a stand of aspens broke across the narrow band of pasture, an obstacle to be negotiated once Kirstie gave the horse her head.

'OK, Kirstie, go!' Matt gave the signal.

She touched Hollywood's sides with her heels. 'Let's start nice and easy!'

Good as gold, the horse responded with a neat, collected trot. Alert to every sound and object on the path ahead, she seemed ready to give her best.

Click-click. 'Let's lope!'

Hollywood broke her tidy trotting rhythm and rolled into a canter, so even and fluid that Kirstie hardly felt the movement. She flexed her legs to keep contact with the saddle, felt the wind whip through her long, fair hair as the horse gathered speed.

The lope became a gallop as they thundered towards the aspens, and yet Hollywood's breathing hardly altered. Her head was stretched forward, her mane flying, feet pounding over the turf.

A rein to the left took them wide of the trees, skimming over a narrow stream that fed the creek.

They were going like the wind, and the freedom
of it, the sheer, beautiful pleasure got to Kirstie.
'Go, Hollywood!' she murmured, leaning low
over her neck, cutting down the wind resistance,
making the most of the horse's amazing burst of
speed.

'Well?' Sandy asked, looking up at Kirstie as she
trotted slowly back to the corral. 'No, don't say
anything. I can see it in your face!'

'Totally . . . !' She was lost for words anyway.
'Brilliant' didn't do it, nor 'fantastic', nor
'fabulous'. Riding Hollywood was all that and
more. *God, I sound like Lisa!* she told herself,
realising how quickly she'd changed her mind
about the horse.

'Well?' Jim Mullins echoed Sandy's question as
he tore his eyes away from the coveted horse.
'What do you say?'

Ben stood by the fence with Charlie. They'd
been joined by Hadley, who'd strolled down from
his cabin to watch Kirstie put Hollywood through
her paces. With their faces partly hidden by the

brims of their stetsons, it was impossible to guess what they were thinking during the long silence that followed the rancher's question.

Kirstie looked from them to Matt and her mom. Absent-mindedly she leaned forward to pat Hollywood's firm, graceful neck. 'Good girl!' she breathed. 'You were great!'

'Wonderful!' Mitzy breathed with an adoring sigh.

The frown of concentration on Sandy Scott's face finally broke. She reached out and took hold of Hollywood's bridle, gently stroked her soft pink muzzle. 'Sorry, Jim, like I said at first, the horse isn't for sale.'

Their neighbour nodded and gave in gracefully. 'Well, I tried.'

'You sure did!' Matt slapped his shoulder in a friendly way. 'Sorry, Jim.'

'I sure would've liked to have her.'

Listening to their neighbour's regrets, Kirstie gave a thumbs-up signal to Ben and the others, then trotted Hollywood into the corral to unsaddle her and brush her down.

'Good decision!' Ben followed her to lend a hand. He and Kirstie slapped palms in a victory salute. 'The way I look at it, the boss did the right thing. Hollywood's an asset the ranch needs to hang on to.'

Kirstie slipped to the ground and watched Ben smoothly slide the saddle from Hollywood's back. 'Yeah, I'm glad,' she agreed, smiling as the mare turned and nudged her with her nose.

'She's a star attraction, that's what she is,' Ben went on. 'You're gonna get guys coming back year after year just to ride this horse!'

'True,' Kirstie nodded. She leaned her cheek against the horse's head. 'But that's not what this is all about, is it, Hollywood?'

'No?' Ben was already busy with a brush and curry comb, but he paused and glanced up at Kirstie.

'No.' Kirstie grinned happily. 'This is about what I'm gonna tell Lisa. The girl would've killed me if we'd sold her favourite horse. I'm telling you straight, I'd have been dead meat!'

* * *

'Hi!' Mitzy Donohoe called out to Kirstie early next morning.

Kirstie had been helping Ben and Charlie bring the horses in from the meadow and was about to slip back into the house to get ready for school. 'Hey,' she mumbled, aware of the fact that she was covered in horse hair, stray wisps of straw and general horse slobber.

Mitzy was immaculate as usual, in her white polo-necked sweater and black English-style jodphurs. She was crossing the yard towards the corral. 'You seen Ben lately?'

'He's in the—' Kirstie began.

'Oh, Ben honey, there you are!' The glamorous guest spotted him and swept on. 'Isn't it a great morning? You hear those birds calling? You see that beautiful pink sky?'

Isn't it a great morning? Waggling her head from side to side, secretly Kirstie mimicked Mitzy's gushing tone. *Ben, honey, there you are!*

'Morning, Mitzy.' Ben was fetching a saddle out of the tack-room. He carried on with his work as the guest leaned on a fence post and surveyed the corral full of restless horses. 'You're up bright and early. We're getting Cadillac ready for you right this minute.'

Stopping to listen, Kirstie realised that the head wrangler was no way as laid back with the dude riders as Hadley had been. He was too polite, too eager.

('Give him time,' her mom had said.)

'Ah, that's what I wanted to talk with you about!' Mitzy picked him up, smooth and bright. 'Cadillac's a fine horse, but I was kinda thinking we should give him a rest today.'

'Well, Mitzy, it's good of you to be paying attention to your horse's welfare,' Ben said. 'I really appreciate that. But these guys are built for stamina. It ain't no problem for Cadillac to keep going day in, day out.'

What's she up to? Kirstie wondered, lingering by the corral. Boy, was she getting suspicious in her old age!

Mitzy heard Ben's answer and changed tack. 'Don't you think it would be good for my riding to use a different horse?'

'Right.' He nodded considerately and walked towards the blackboard where horses and riders were matched. 'Good point. You want me to see who's free?'

Mitzy slipped through the gate and joined Ben on the tack-room porch. She pointed to the list. 'Hollywood!'

That's it! Kirstie realised. Mitzy was up early expressly to grab a ride on the prettiest horse in the ramuda. And, though it smacked of reserving the best poolside position and hogging it for the entire day, after yesterday's dream ride, Kirstie could hardly blame the quick-thinking guest.

'Well now, Hollywood Princess is quite a handful.' Ben hesitated and kept on studying the list. 'Maybe you'd be better off with Snowflake here.'

'Are you saying I can't handle Hollywood?' Mitzy argued back. The smile had suddenly slipped, replaced by a small frown.

'No, ma'am. All I'm saying is the horse has plenty of juice and maybe she ain't quite ready for a trail-ride.'

'*You* rode her!' Mitzy pointed out. She looked sideways at Ben, then slid into another tone that Kirstie recognised. 'Plee-ase!' she wheedled. 'I'll be OK on Hollywood, I promise!'

The wrangler weakened immediately under the velvet pressure. 'OK, you win,' he told her, chalking her name into the empty box. 'You get to ride our star horse.'

Mitzy's triumphant smile as she jumped down from the porch said it all. So did Hadley's grunt from across the yard.

'You hear that?' Kirstie asked the old man, rushing towards the house now because she'd made herself late.

'Sure did.'

'What d'you think?'

'It don't matter what I think,' he mumbled, walking off up the hill to his cabin. 'But those are darn silly pants that gal is wearing. Why can't she put on a decent pair of jeans like the rest of us?'

5

'And guess what!' Kirstie grinned at Lisa. 'Hollywood behaved like an angel for a day and a half. She stayed tucked in behind Ben and Cadillac, ignoring all the crazy stuff Mitzy was trying to get her to do.'

The two girls were sitting cross-legged on Kirstie's bed. It was late Friday and they were looking forward to a Saturday of bushwhacking across country with saddle-bags stocked up with sandwiches, chips and Hershey bars; a lazy, free day in the mountains. But meanwhile, Kirstie was filling her friend in on the week's events at the ranch.

'And then what?' Lisa wanted to hear the end of the Mitzy-Hollywood saga.

'And then this afternoon, on the way back to the ranch by Five Mile Creek, Ms Donohoe gave one kick, one tug on the reins too many – whatever. Anyway, Hollywood said, *This is too much!*'

'What did she do?'

Kirstie's mouth twitched. 'She dumped her rider!'

'No! Where?'

'In the creek.'

'Oh, wow! Really?' Lisa began to giggle.

'Yeah. Imagine it; according to Charlie, Hollywood stops in her tracks like this!' Jumping up, Kirstie imitated a horse digging in its heels and refusing to budge. Slowly, deliberately she turned her head to stare at her invisible rider. 'Mitzy gets mad at her and digs her hard with her heels. Hollywood gives a big sigh, like, *What is this woman like!* She takes a couple of steps down the bank and stands knee deep in water.'

'God, Kirstie, I can just see Mitzy's face!'

'OK, she's sitting on a horse that's standing in a foot of running water and she panics.'

'Bad idea!' Lisa laughed.

'So she kicks some more. By this time, of course, Hollywood can't feel it. She only knows she wants to get rid of this thing on her back.'

'Good for her!'

'She's in the creek, knowing that everyone in the group is staring at her, wondering what the heck she's gonna do next. And you know what she's like when she hogs the limelight. She shows off.' Kirstie was enjoying every moment of the reconstruction, as told to her by Charlie.

'Come on, tell me exactly what happened!'

Kirstie delayed for a few seconds, struggling to keep her face straight. 'Hollywood just goes right ahead and does her Lone Ranger trick. She rears, Mitzy hangs on to the horn ... Hollywood prances, the rider slips ... backwards, backwards, and she's let go, she's sliding off over Hollywood's rump . . . splash into the creek!'

'Was she hurt?'

'Yeah.' Kirstie nodded gravely. 'A bad case of injured pride. They scooped her out and took her home to her cabin. An hour in the hot-tub and she was fine.'

'Lucky,' Lisa sighed.

Kirstie agreed. 'She could've broken an arm or a leg, easy.'

'No, I mean lucky for me.' Plumping up the pillows on Kirstie's bed, Lisa lay back with her arms behind her head. 'Mitzy's accident means no way will she be wanting to use Hollywood again, which means—'

'You can ride her tomorrow!' Kirstie guessed.

'Dream come true!' Lisa sighed. 'A whole day on the most gorgeous horse in the world!'

Away from the crowd, bushwhacking with Kirstie and Lucky, Hollywood gave Lisa the time of her life.

She was sturdy and steady on the long pull up

Meltwater Trail to Miners' Ridge, fearless through the shadows and overhanging cliffs of Dead Man's Canyon.

'Maybe I've been too hard on her,' Kirstie conceded as she and Lucky picked their way up a narrow track next to a tumbling waterfall. 'When she first came, I had her down as an attention seeker plain and simple.'

'And now?' Lisa held Hollywood back until Lucky had made it to the next ledge. They stopped in a patch of dappled sunlight, looking up at a smooth ridge of bare granite called Hummingbird Rock.

'Now I think she just loves life!' Kirstie's reply was partly smothered by the crash of water into the fall. She looked down at the swirl of white water in a pool twenty feet below. 'That way of picking up her feet and strutting is saying, "Isn't life great? Isn't this an amazing place to be?" '

Lisa urged Hollywood on to join Lucky. 'Hey, don't you go falling in love with "my" horse, you hear!'

Kirstie grinned, leaning forward to pat her palomino's solid, golden neck. 'And desert this guy? Never!'

Over Hummingbird Rock and on to Bear Hunt Overlook without seeing a single soul. Only the tiny round hummingbirds with the long, pointed beaks sucking nectar from the blue columbines growing at the base of the aspen trees. Only the ground squirrels with their striped tails, stalked by the red fox whose white tail tip gave him away as he crept along a decaying log and pounced too late.

Kirstie and Lucky, Lisa and Hollywood Princess roamed the whole day, only resting during the heat of the midday sun, when the horses took shelter in the shade of tall pines. Then they went on into the late afternoon, returning by Eden Lake and along Five Mile Creek.

'Heaven!' Lisa sighed. They were within sight of Half-Moon Ranch. She and Hollywood had got so used to one another that she only had to pass on the slightest command with leg or rein to get the horse to switch from walk to trot, or to turn to left and right.

Kirstie glanced at them now, as they picked their way across a stream and through the stand of aspens where she'd galloped Hollywood for Jim Mullins earlier in the week. As ever, she was struck by the sheer beauty of the white horse, her daintiness, her grace. 'If that was heaven, are you ready for a return to reality?' she asked.

'Nope!' Lisa wove in and out of the slender, silver-barked trees. Sunlight played on Hollywood's smooth white coat, making the threads of her silky mane gleam.

'You'd better be!' Kirstie warned, looking ahead to a bustle of activity at the ranch. She could see horses tethered in the corral, a crowd of people gathered by the round-pen. 'We got back just in time for the Fun Rodeo!'

'Charlie, set up that loudspeaker system over there by the tack-room door!' Ben yelled. 'And Matt, can you get the contestants for the barrel race to line up in the corral?'

The head wrangler wore a hassled look as he ran from place to place, issuing orders and making sure that everything was in place for the rodeo to begin.

'Hey, Kirstie! Hey, Lisa!' Sandy Scott greeted the girls as they rode into the yard. Dressed in a crisp pale blue shirt and jeans, she let the fuss and hurry pass her by. 'Did you have a good ride?'

As Lisa stopped to tell her all about it, Kirstie rode Lucky on into the corral. She'd forgotten until the last minute that late Saturday was the time for the week's guests to come together and have some fun, wild west style. There would be a barrel race for the kids, a game of tag, some fooling around by the wranglers with ropes and lassos, all finished off by a quarter-mile sprint race for the ranch staff along the side of the creek. Afterwards, they would set up a barbecue by the footbridge: grilled chicken, jacket potatoes and sweetcorn.

'Charlie, I want the table for the microphone here, not over there!' Ben had changed his mind without telling anyone, causing a confusion that

Charlie and Matt had to sort out between them.

'What can I do?' Kirstie offered, tethering Lucky and bracing herself to help.

'Make a list of the names for the sprint and give it to Mitzy.' Ben threw her a job, rushing past Hadley and Jim Mullins who had come to chew the fat with his old friend.

Kirstie grabbed pen and paper from the newly set-up table. 'You want to enter?' she asked Hadley with a cheeky grin.

The old man closed one eye and squinted at her with the other. 'You saying I couldn't if I wanted to?'

'No, never!' she assured him. 'What's one more broken bone here or there, hey, Hadley?' The old cowboy was fond of telling people how he'd bust every bone in his body in his time.

'Write my name down!' he said now, taking up the teasing challenge. 'I'll ride Rodeo Rocky and whup everyone half my age!'

'Crazy!' Jim Mullins laughed and shook his head. He backed off from Kirstie's enquiring gaze. 'No way, kiddo; leave me out of this!'

'Wise move!' Sandy told him, passing by with microphone and speakers.

'Mom, I've put you down to ride Jitterbug.' Kirstie seized her chance and didn't wait for a response. Instead, she hurried on to tell Matt that he was riding his own horse, Cadillac, in the sprint, and Charlie that he could have Johnny Mohawk because Hadley was already down to ride Rocky.

'Hadley?' Charlie echoed in surprise.

'Sure. Why not?' Kirstie was busy writing. 'He only retired from his job as head wrangler, didn't he? That doesn't mean he has to go doddery and feeble on us! Now, Ben, you have a choice of Snowflake or Navaho Joe.' She sped on across the corral to accost her next victim. 'Navaho Joe would be best.'

'You're on Lucky,' Ben reminded her. 'You're in there too, remember!'

She jotted down her own name.

'And I'm on Hollywood Princess,' Lisa muttered over her shoulder.

'You sure?' Kirstie hesitated, pen poised. The

staff sprint race was likely to be tough, fast and rough.

'Sure!' her friend insisted, eyes gleaming, face eager. 'No way are you leaving me and Hollywood out!'

'That's where the quarter horse got its name,' Ben explained to a bunch of guest kids. The barrel race had been run and won by a twelve-year-old girl from Texas. Now he was setting up the start point for the final event of the evening: the four-hundred-and-forty-yard dash by the side of Five Mile Creek.

'How? I don't get it.' Jack, the seven-year-old brother of the Texan winner, Carole-Ann Mitchell, kept doggedly at it, question after question. 'Why is a quarter horse called a quarter horse?'

'Because they ran races over a quarter of a mile, stupid!' his sister told him.

'That's right.' Despite the hassle of the afternoon's activities, Ben still found time for the puzzled kid. 'In the old days, they'd set up a rodeo event in an arena, roping and bull-dogging steers. Then, at the end of the day, the cowboys would lay bets and set off in a race around the outside of the arena, which was roughly a quarter of a mile from start to finish. Those horses were tough. They took off like bullets, didn't hardly draw breath until they broke through the finishing tape.'

'Wow, I wish I'd seen that!' Jack was impressed.

Ben grinned at him, lifted him clean off his feet and sat him on top of a stack of hay bales, where he could see over the heads of the grown-ups and bigger kids gathered for the start of the race. 'You stay right there!' he told him. 'What you're gonna see now is ten times better than the old sprint races. You wait!'

Kirstie had stood by with Ben's horse, the brown and white Appaloosa, Navaho Joe. Joe had a wild streak and had spent the late fall up on Eagle's Peak, refusing to be tempted down by food or shelter. 'You stand a good chance,' she confided in Ben as he took the reins and swung up into the saddle. 'Stay on the outside, away from the creek. He likes plenty of space.'

'You bet!' Thanking her, he trotted to the start line to join Sandy on Jitterbug, Charlie on Johnny Mohawk and Matt on Cadillac.

'Go, Ben!' a voice from the crowd called. It was Mitzy Donohoe, fully recovered from her unexpected dip and whipping up excitement amongst the spectators.

'Yeah, go Ben!' Jack Mitchell joined in.

'Ready, Kirstie?' Lisa came out of the corral on Hollywood, leading Lucky on a short rope.

'Sure.' Kirstie took the rope and looped it, knotting it to the side of the saddle with two leather thongs. She was halfway into the saddle when Lisa reminded her that she'd forgotten her hat, so she went quickly to the tack-room where she'd last worn it.

'You seen my hat?' she asked Hadley, who was tying on his beaten-up chaps, refusing to hurry for the start of the race.

'Nope,' he muttered, then strode out to find his horse.

'Thanks, Hadley!' Kirstie sighed, spinning round and grabbing the only stetson she could find. It was a couple of sizes too big, but it would have to do.

Running back to the corral, she vaulted into Lucky's saddle and followed Hadley and Rodeo Rocky out to the starting-point.

'Ready!' Jim Mullins stood to one side, red flag in hand.

Strung out in a straight row from left to right, there was Ben on Joe, Matt on Cadillac, Charlie on Johnny Mohawk, fighting to keep his horse in line. The black stallion skittered sideways in his eagerness, tossing his head and shaking his wild, dark mane. Then came Sandy on Jitterbug, Lisa on Hollywood. Kirstie decided to squeeze Lucky between her and Hadley on Rocky. She noticed that the wily old wrangler had chosen the inside position for the ex-rodeo horse – a neat idea, since the course followed the creek, which bent slightly to the right.

'Get set!' Jim's flag was poised. He waited for the horses to stop jostling and concentrate their minds on the quarter-of-a-mile stretch of ground ahead.

'OK, Lucky!' Kirstie leaned forward and breathed in his ear. 'This next thirty seconds is gonna be wild, I'm telling you!'

His ears flicked, he set his head forward, bunched his muscles, ready to sprint.

'Go!' Jim's voice boomed and the flag came down.

'Go, Ben, go!' Mitzy led a chant for the new head wrangler, whose pretty Appie shot ahead in the first two seconds.

The seven horses thundered away, kicking up dirt, jostling for position.

'Yee-hah!' Matt yelled, getting into a neck-to-neck race with his great friend, Charlie.

Little Johnny Mohawk was having none of it. He matched long-legged Cadillac stride for stride.

Out of the corner of her eye, Kirstie could see Ben riding wide on Joe, losing ground now to Sandy and Jitterbug. But Jitterbug didn't have the stamina, she knew. To her right, Hadley was doing pretty well on Rocky, steering him clear of the creek, not wasting an inch of ground.

'C'mon, Lucky!' Kirstie urged, bent low over his neck, keeping pace with both Lisa on her left and Hadley to her right.

The brave palomino gave her all he had. Fifteen seconds into the race and half way down the course, he was half a length ahead of Rocky, a full length in front of Hollywood.

But the dust kicked up by Jitterbug and Joe was drifting sideways into Matt and Charlie's faces, then lodging in Lisa and Kirstie's eyes. It stung sharply, forcing Kirstie to duck her head. When she raised it again, the wind caught the brim of her hat and whipped it clean off her head.

It vanished with a flap and a whoosh, whirling away. The sudden flying object caught Hollywood full in the face, making her veer off to the right in panic.

Kirstie heard the break in the galloping rhythm of the white horse's hooves. She caught the edge of Lisa's sudden cry and turned in time to see Hollywood rearing on to her hind legs, her front hooves high in the air, her mouth open and squealing in fright.

'Lisa!' Kirstie called her friend's name.

There was a moment frozen in time. A beat of hooves as five horses galloped on, a picture of Hollywood raised up on her strong hind legs, of Lisa's whole body being whipped back by the force of gravity, her hands grasping for the saddle horn, losing it, sliding backwards. Then she was flung sideways as the horse plunged and swung round.

Lisa's feet came out of the saddle; her body was limp as a rag doll as she was thrown and landed.

There was a thud, then stillness.

But Hollywood was still kicking and rearing. Then she headed off-balance towards the creek, stumbling down the rocky bank on to her knees, crying out in pain. Water splashed as she fell sideways then tried to struggle up. She went down again on her side, her head sinking into the rushing stream.

'Lisa!' Kirstie was down from Lucky's saddle,

running, pleading with her to get up.

Lisa lay on her back, her face white and turned awkwardly to one side, eyes closed. Yellow dirt clogged her bright red curls and a thin trail of blood trickled from the corner of her mouth on to the crushed, filthy hat wedged under her shoulder.

6

'. . . They called him Chuck-chuck, see?' Lisa lay
in a hospital bed, her broken collar bone and
dislocated hip protected by wire cages which lifted
the bedclothes clear of her body. She wore a neck-
brace to keep her head in position until the
swelling around the vertebrae reduced. Then the
radiographer would X-ray the spine and check
for hairline fractures or any other damage to the
bones which protected the vital spinal cord.

Kirstie shook her head. 'Don't try to talk,' she pleaded.

'Hey, *talking* is about all I can do!' her friend protested, her face still almost as pale as the sheets covering her bruised and broken body. 'My mom just read me a piece from the *Readers Digest*. It said that this kid's name was Guy Chicken, and all the other kids called him Chuck-chuck!'

'Please!' Kirstie thought that this conversation was a bad idea. She wanted Lisa to stay as quiet and still as possible.

'No, listen!' Though she could hardly move a muscle, the patient was determined to put on a brave face. 'So, Guy's parents thought he shouldn't have to take any more hassle, so they decided to change the family name to use his mom's name before marriage.'

'So?' Kirstie was hardly listening. The sight of her best friend all strapped up, her head bruised, surrounded by charts and all the horrible hospital stuff, had sent her head spinning.

'So, his mom's name was Barker. He became Guy Barker!'

'Yeah?' She tuned in for the punch line.

'Guy Barker. The poor kid goes into school next day, and the rats in his class don't call him Chuck-chuck any longer. What they say is, "Hey, Woof-woof, how're you doin'?" Get it? Barker . . . dog . . . Woof-woof!'

Kirstie managed to raise a smile. 'Hey, listen, Lisa, I need to say I'm—'

'Don't!' Suddenly serious, Lisa made as if to raise her head from the pillow. 'Definitely do not!'

'But . . .' All night Kirstie had lain awake telling herself that this would never have happened if she hadn't been wearing a hat that was too big for her. She should have realised . . . taken more care . . . never picked the stetson up in the first place. What she needed to tell Lisa was that she was sorry.

'No, really, Kirstie; don't say anything!' Lisa's eyes had filled with tears and she turned her head away towards the window. When she looked back, she'd got a grip again. 'There's just one thing bothering me.'

Kirstie swallowed hard and nodded.

Lisa's pale face was drawn and anxious. Despite her brave front, the shadowy smudges under her eyes conveyed the real trauma of the accident. 'Listen, no one's saying that this was down to Hollywood, are they?'

Hastily Kirstie shook her head. She wanted to keep the subject away from the white horse. ''Course not.'

'Because I know what guys are like. If something bad like this happens, they need someone to blame. My mom already tried it. She was saying that no way should the ranch have let me ride a new horse without the wranglers having worked her in first.'

Kirstie frowned and glanced down the ward to where Bonnie Goodman stood deep in conversation with a nurse. The Scotts and the Goodmans went way back, and she knew that Lisa's mom was a down-to-earth, easy-going type. Yet here she was, blaming Half-Moon Ranch for her daughter's accident. Maybe that was only natural, as Lisa said.

'I told her: "Hey, Mom, what're you talkin'

about? You weren't even there!" ' Picking up Kirstie's unease, Lisa tried to return to her earlier jokey style. 'You know my mom. According to her, a wooden rocking-horse is a lethal weapon! No, really, Kirstie, I want you to stand up for Hollywood if they try to dump this on her!'

Kirstie agreed. 'If it's down to anyone it's down to me,' she muttered.

'No way!' Once more Lisa tried to raise her head. 'It was a freak accident, pure and simple!'

This time, it was Kirstie's turn to feel her eyes fill up with tears. Sensing through her blurred vision that Bonnie Goodman was on her way down the ward, she felt that it was time to leave. 'I'll be back soon, if that's OK with you.'

'Sure. I'm not going anywhere!'

Returning her friend's brave smile, Kirstie was about to beat a retreat. But one last question, the one she'd been dreading since the start of the visit, stopped her in her tracks.

'Kirstie, you gotta tell me: how is Hollywood?'

Kirstie closed her eyes and turned back

towards the bed. 'Glen Woodford's taking good care of her.'

Lisa's eyes wouldn't let her get away with this.

'He's the best vet around,' Kirstie insisted.

Still those green eyes bored into her.

'We got him out to the ranch just as soon as we could. He was there within half an hour of the accident.' Kirstie floundered on with her explanation. Sooner or later, she would be forced to deliver the facts. 'Matt knew what to do, of course. He gave first-aid until Glen arrived, recognised that the horse was in shock, handed out the orders to the rest of us—'

'How *is* she?' Lisa pleaded.

By this time, Bonnie had reached her daughter's bedside and had begun to fuss with the pillows.

'She has a puncture wound in her chest, she tore the skin off both her knees, and Glen thinks there's a bad sprain to her flexor tendon just above the rear right fetlock.'

'Is that it? Nothing broken?'

'Glen reckons not.'

Lisa closed her eyes and sighed. 'Thank God!'

Bonnie moved around the bed, whispering to Kirstie as she passed by, 'Lisa needs to rest.'

Nodding, promising again to come back soon, Kirstie said goodbye.

''Bye.' Wearily Lisa opened her eyes once more. Then, 'Hollywood is OK, isn't she?'

'Yeah,' Kirstie replied with a heavy heart. She'd delivered the facts as far as she knew them, but she hadn't told Lisa the whole truth. 'Don't you worry, Hollywood is gonna be just fine!'

The truth was, they were all seriously worried about the injured horse.

'There's more to break than just bones,' Glen Woodford had confided to Sandy Scott after he'd treated the wounds and given Hollywood the anti-tetanus booster and antibiotic shots she needed. 'There's the will to get better; that's very important in an animal – any animal – but especially one like Hollywood Princess, who's used to being at the centre of things.'

Kirstie had listened and understood perfectly

as the broad-shouldered, quietly spoken vet had outlined the prognosis for the patient. She recalled when Lucky was ill, how it had been sheer willpower that had got him through the worst. That and her own belief in the healing powers of Zak Stone, the legendary horse doctor who lived in a log cabin deep in the Rockies. That journey to see him and have him treat Lucky's illness had taken every ounce of energy and faith that both she and Lucky possessed.

'Don't worry, Hollywood will get plenty of tender loving care,' Sandy had promised the vet, standing in the quiet yard outside the house once the drama of the accident and the arrival of the ambulance from Denver had died down. By this time it had been sunset, and Hollywood had been bedded down in a quiet stall.

The torn flesh on her knees had been sutured, along with the chest wound. Glen had advised Matt to keep the knees bandaged but the chest wound open. 'It goes pretty deep,' he warned. 'If you cover it, you may get abscesses. Soap it daily to remove scabs, and wash it out with

Betadine antiseptic solution.'

Matt had fetched the ranch's health programme records from the office and checked that Hollywood's inoculations were in order.

'And don't quit bandaging the knees too early,' Glen had warned. 'Those wounds will take between seven and ten days to drain. After that, you keep on with the proud flesh ointment and the bandages until the edges of the skin have had time to grow together.'

'So not too much of a scar?' Sandy had asked.

Glen had held up crossed fingers and climbed into his Jeep with a sympathetic smile at Kirstie. 'And don't let her put weight on that tendon sprain!' he'd ordered. 'No Lone Ranger tricks for the foreseeable future, OK?'

She'd smiled weakly and promised, wishing that her head would stop whirling, thinking even then, *This is my fault! My friend is being hospitalised right this minute and a horse is in danger, and it's all down to me!*

'Lisa's gonna be OK,' Sandy promised Kirstie on

the ride back from Denver City General to the ranch.

People said these things to make you feel better, but they were never very convincing. Kirstie gave one of those vague half-smiles she'd been using a lot since the accident and turned to look out of the window. Way in the distance she recognised the conical, white-capped shape of Eagle's Peak against a clear, eggshell-blue sky.

'Bonnie could do without this, though,' her mom murmured, taking the exit off the interstate on to Route 5. 'I don't know how she's gonna run the diner and visit Lisa in hospital all at the same time.'

They sat in silence for a while, recognising the impossibility of Bonnie's situation.

'Lisa said her mom blames Hollywood—' Kirstie began in a low, mumbling voice.

'Bonnie said the accident was down to Ben—' Sandy muttered at the same time.

'Sorry.'

'No, go ahead.' Sandy glanced at Kirstie, then back at the winding, narrow road.

'Bonnie reckons the horse spooked too easily, I guess.' She voiced her deep concern.

'The way I heard it, Ben should've been the one to ride Hollywood, not Lisa. Bonnie says the head wrangler should check out a horse thoroughly before he hands it over to someone else.' Kirstie's mom sighed and shook her head. 'I told her that in the end I'm the one who takes responsibility for everything that goes on at the ranch. If she's looking to blame anybody, it had better be me.'

This was like going down a maze without being able to find the exit. Maybe it was best to see it the way Lisa did, as a pure freak accident. Kirstie's mind went back to the moment when the hat had flown off her head, and she relived the following five minutes in vivid detail.

Lisa unconscious, the yellow dirt in her hair, the thin trail of blood.

Matt dismounting from Cadillac and sprinting back fifty yards to the scene of the accident, yelling at Kirstie not to lift Lisa, not even to touch her.

He'd run one way to help Hollywood, Sandy had

come to take care of the unconscious girl.

Kirstie standing up and backing away from her friend. Stumbling down the bank of the creek, splashing through the water to crouch beside Matt.

Hollywood's beautiful white head half-submerged, blood from the punctured artery pumping into the clear stream.

Matt had shouted for first-aid equipment from the tack-room, there had been figures running here and there, he'd pressed the wound in the horse's chest with his bare hands until someone brought a pad of lint to staunch the bleeding.

So much blood. Scarlet on white.

Hollywood had come round and tried to raise herself. Like Lisa from her hospital bed.

The horse's long mane had streamed with blood-stained water. Her eyes had rolled with fear as she staggered to her feet, driving away those who were trying to help. She'd stood, knees broken, causing the chest wound to flow again. And she'd tried to beat them back the best way she knew, by resting her whole weight back and raising her front hooves to paw the air – her Lone Ranger trick.

But the back leg had given way and she'd staggered and fallen.

Ben had run forward to grab her reins, Matt had moved in again. Between them they'd calmed her and stopped the bleeding once more.

While an ambulance came for Lisa, Glen Woodford drove out from San Luis to tend to Hollywood. No bones broken. Sutures and dressings. A return to normality.

But Glen's words came back to her. 'There's more to a break than just bones . . . there's the will to get better . . .' Did Hollywood have any fight left in her?

And now they were home after the hospital visit. Kirstie had given Lisa the facts but not the truth. Blame was ricocheting around like pieces of shrapnel from a bomb blast. Hollywood Princess was in a stall in the quiet barn, suffering the aftermath.

'Hey,' Kirstie murmured.

She went into the stall, hearing her feet rustle through the deep straw.

Hollywood lay on her side in the corner, looking up as Kirstie entered. Her dark eyes were listless, her head seemed heavy and uncontrollable as she tried to lift it. The bandaging on her knees kept her front legs straight and stiff, the sutures across her chest looked painfully raw.

Here in the dark and quiet, Kirstie had a flash of Hollywood strutting and prancing in front of Jim Mullins, of her dancing and shimmying to impress Johnny Mohawk – of Hollywood the pin-up horse.

And here she was now, a white ghost of her former self, lying helpless and sedated, wounds throbbing with pain, the back leg swollen out of shape.

Kirstie knelt beside her and stroked her neck. For a moment she was angry with Hollywood for not being the way she should be. *Where's your sassy self-confidence? Why aren't you out there proving to the world that you're indestructible?*

And then there were tears in her eyes, rolling down her cheeks as she stroked the smooth white neck and ran her fingers through the long, tangled mane.

Hollywood sighed and looked at her with dark eyes that were full of pain and confusion.

'I'm sorry!' Kirstie whispered. 'So, so sorry!'

7

'Howdy, Tony! You done much riding before?'

It was Sunday afternoon in the corral. Ben was addressing a new bunch of riders waiting in the line-up for a horse. Twelve visitors, including Mitzy Donohoe, had left and fourteen new ones had arrived. The life of the dude ranch went on regardless.

'Sure. I've been horseback riding since I was a little kid,' the man replied. 'This is my sixth visit to Half-Moon Ranch, as a matter of fact.'

Hadley would've known that, Kirstie thought. After an hour with Hollywood Princess in the barn, she'd come out to face the routine of everyday living.

Ben gave an embarrassed nod and cough, then chalked Tony's name up alongside Moose.

Looking a mite disappointed by Ben's choice of the steady, big-boned grey gelding, Tony nevertheless shuffled off to be fitted for a saddle.

And Hadley would never have given him Moose, was Kirstie's next criticism. It seemed that the accident with Hollywood had made the new head wrangler more cautious and less confident than ever.

He went on to the next guest, a tough-looking kid who was chewing gum and making his own decisions.

'Gimme Johnny Mohawk,' he told Ben. 'That's the horse I rode last fall.'

Ben frowned, then nodded. Without giving the kid any argument, he chalked another name on the board.

'Don't say a word!' Matt muttered under his breath as he strode by, noting the inconsistency of Ben's method. 'Hey, Kirstie, Lisa's on the phone for you.'

'Right now?' It was only three hours since she and Sandy had left the hospital.

'Sure, right now.' Matt hurried on towards the barn, obviously planning to check on Hollywood.

So Kirstie ran to take the call, steeling herself for more questions about Hollywood. And sure enough, that was Lisa's first topic of conversation from her hospital bed.

'So,' she demanded, 'how is she?'

'How's who?'

'Quit stalling, Kirstie. Did you see her since you got back?'

'Yes, I just spent an hour with her.' Still she hesitated over how to shape her answer.

'She's real bad, isn't she?' Lisa interpreted the pauses correctly. 'C'mon, give it to me straight!'

'It's like I told you: Glen stitched her up and made her comfortable—'

'So how come you sound like you just went to a

funeral?' This time around, Lisa was determined to squeeze more out of Kirstie.

'Because . . . because, I'm worried about her, I guess!' She blurted it out. 'Lisa, you wouldn't know her if you saw her. I mean, she just isn't the horse we know!'

Lisa took a while to absorb the answer. 'I knew it was bad,' she muttered, her voice thin and strained. 'You're the worst liar, Kirstie Scott!'

'Sorry. I didn't want to give you any more of a problem than you've already got. And anyway, it could be a reaction to the tetanus booster, or she could still be traumatised by the accident. Tomorrow she might be one hundred per cent better!' For Lisa's sake she tried to look on the bright side.

'Yeah, maybe.'

There was another long pause, which Kirstie broke by changing the subject. 'So, what's new with you?'

'They decided to put my hip back in place later today.'

'Ouch! How do they do that?'

'They give me a painkiller and the physios manipulate it into the socket. My doctor says I have very supple joints. He's kinda cute.' Lisa's attempt at cheeriness faded into silence again.

'What about your collar bone?' Kirstie asked.

'They put that in a brace to immobilise it and eventually it mends itself.'

'Did they X-ray your spine yet?'

'Nope. Too much swelling. Hey, listen; you don't get me off the subject of Hollywood so easy! I want to know what you really think!'

'I already told you. Listen, Lisa, I gotta go!' What else was there to say? 'Give me a call after school tomorrow, OK?'

'OK.' She was fainter than before; there was a sense of feeling let down in her voice which she made no attempt to disguise. 'Say hello to Hollywood for me, would you, please?'

'Yeah, sure. You take care, OK?' Kirstie dropped the phone on to its cradle, turning to find her mom standing quietly in the doorway. She felt her bottom lip begin to tremble.

'Hey, daughter, what do we do round here when

we find ourselves caught between a rock and a hard place?' Sandy asked gently, without altering her position.

Kirstie squared her shoulders and sniffed. 'We cowboy up!' she reminded herself weakly.

'That's what we do,' Sandy confirmed with a brief, firm nod.

After all, there were horses to saddle for the new riders, trail-rides to lead. And Lucky to talk to when the going got really, really tough.

'No way should you have let my girl ride that horse!' Bonnie Goodman's voice was raised against Ben.

It was Tuesday evening, three days after Lisa's accident, and her mom was on the warpath. She'd forsaken the End of Trail Diner and driven out to the ranch to give the new head wrangler a piece of her mind.

'Mrs Goodman, what can I tell you? I'm real sorry about what happened . . .' Ben already looked caved in by the confrontation, which happened as soon as Bonnie had got out of her car. She'd made straight for the tack-room and laid into the man she held responsible. 'Lisa loved riding Hollywood. She'd been out on her all day before the accident.'

'Exactly!' Bonnie raised her voice higher still. 'Your job is to supervise what goes on. Yet you allow my girl out of your sight on a horse you know nothing about . . .' Ending in an exasperated splutter, she appealed to onlookers for support.

Charlie, who had heard the beginning of the row, retreated with a shrug to a dark corner. Kirstie, just back from school, didn't move quick enough.

'It's true, ain't it?' Bonnie appealed to Kirstie, her wide, round face turning red with rising frustration.

'Ben's knowledge of Hollywood Princess goes way back, actually. And we took a two-way radio with us, like we always do,' Kirstie pointed out. 'Lisa's a good rider, Mrs Goodman.' Her natural sense of justice made her want to paint the true picture. 'She took to Hollywood right away. It would've been hard to stop her riding the horse. Even Hadley couldn't have done it, I reckon!'

Bonnie frowned and turned back to Ben. 'It's your job here to ensure the safety of all riders! My girl's lying in a hospital bed because you didn't do that properly. The way I see it, it's down to you!'

Kirstie saw Ben clench his jaw tight and look down at the dusty floorboards. Something made him draw back from arguing his case any further and she wasn't sure what it was exactly. 'You gotta listen,' she implored on his behalf, stepping forward between Bonnie and Ben. 'It wasn't Ben here that made the decision about Lisa riding Hollywood; it was me!'

'Then you're as bad as he is!' Bonnie turned on her in a kind of fizz of exasperation, shooting off in all directions. 'You're so crazy about horses, Kirstie Scott, it blinds you to reason. You forget that this is twelve hundred pounds of solid muscle and bone we're talking about, and very little brain!'

Kirstie took a breath, then changed her mind. Like Ben before her, she stepped back from the argument. After all, Bonnie already had enough on her plate.

To everyone's relief, Sandy Scott chose this moment to walk into the tack-room. In an instant she took in the tension of the situation: Bonnie's face flushed with anger, Ben looking dejectedly at the floor, Charlie hovering in a far corner. 'I saw your car in the yard,' she told Bonnie. 'I came to find out the latest news on Lisa.'

'They X-rayed her spine,' Bonnie said, her voice flat as she turned away from Ben and Kirstie.

'And?' Sandy came forward with a protective gesture, taking her distraught friend by the hand.

Kirstie closed her eyes and prayed.

'They say it's OK!' Bonnie whispered, breaking down for the first time since the accident and leaning against Sandy's shoulder. 'They're gonna keep her in hospital a couple more days, then they're gonna let her come home!'

'So that's good news,' Kirstie said to Lisa on the phone. She'd rung the hospital as soon as Bonnie had let them know the result of the X-rays.

'Listen, honey, it takes more than a little old fall to finish me off!' Lisa sounded almost back to her old self. 'Hey, my mom isn't over there giving you a hard time by any chance?'

Kirstie laughed. 'You could say that.'

'Take no notice, you hear? Her bark is worse than her bite.'

'Tell that to Ben!' Kirstie saw him now through the window, showing Glen Woodford into the barn. From a distance, the wrangler looked very down indeed.

'Explain that she sounds off without really meaning it sometimes,' Lisa went on. 'Oh, and before you go, I want you to promise me that by the time I get out of this place, you and Ben will get Hollywood back on her feet, ready to greet me!'

Immediately Kirstie tensed up, gripping the phone tight and choking over her reply.

'Hey, friend, you still there?'

'Yeah. Listen, Lisa. About Hollywood—'

'What is it? If it's bad news, tell me quick!' Lisa gabbled. 'Did she die?'

'No. No, she's alive and kicking. Glen's here with her right this minute.'

'Which means what?'

Kirstie swallowed hard. 'It means she's still sick. She didn't bounce back like we hoped.'

When she hadn't been at school, Kirstie had spent every spare moment with the sick horse: talking to her, encouraging her to eat, making sure that her bedding was clean and comfortable. She'd watched with an eagle eye for any sign of improvement, helping Matt, Sandy or Ben change the bandages and keep the chest wound clean.

But rather than get better, Hollywood seemed to be sliding slowly downhill. Ben had spotted a swelling on her hind leg, where she'd damaged the tendon, and he'd noticed that the swollen fetlock joint was hot and inflamed. That was why he'd called Glen Woodford back, and it was what was worrying Kirstie right now.

'I don't believe it!' From sounding almost bubbly about her own situation, Lisa had fallen into a tone of near-panic. 'Kirstie, say you're kidding me!'

'No. It's true. Hollywood isn't doing too good.'
She wished with all her heart she could be saying
the opposite: that Hollywood would be there at
the gate of Red Fox Meadow when Lisa next
called, that she would be her old glamorous self
strutting her stuff.

'Then *make* her!' Lisa insisted.

'How?' How, for heaven's sake, did you force a
horse to recover from an injury?

'I don't know how. You tell me!' Lisa was almost
yelling down the phone, then her voice broke and
she was pleading. 'You can do it, Kirstie. You made
Lucky get well, didn't you?'

'But that was different.' Lucky and she had a
bond that no one could break, a trust that had
built up over five whole years.

'No, it's the same,' Lisa sobbed. 'You know how
much Hollywood means to me, don't you?'

'Yes.' And worse, Kirstie still felt responsible
for what had happened during the race. Knowing
deep down what Lisa was about to ask, she also
realised what her answer must be.

'So, if you really are my friend,' Lisa managed

to murmur between sobs, 'you'll try as hard as ever you can to get her well again, won't you?'

'It sure is a shame,' Glen Woodford said as he knelt over the sick horse. 'I hate to see an animal go down so fast.'

Kirstie had gone straight over to the barn after her phone call with Lisa, hoping against hope that the vet would give them some good news. But Ben's face as he glanced up told her a different story.

And now Glen himself was confirming that Hollywood's condition had worsened.

In fact, if she was honest, Kirstie could see it for herself. Not eating and lying in the stall since the accident meant Hollywood had lost weight and muscle. Her silky white coat had turned dull and scurfy, her eyes were sunken, her whole attitude apathetic.

'You see how depressed she is.' Glen pointed out the way her head sank against the straw, and how she took no interest in the ultrasonic equipment he'd been using to try to reduce the swelling above her fetlock.

Ben nodded and passed his hand over his forehead. 'Should we hose down the joint to cool it down?'

'Sure, as often as you can. Now that the chest wound has started to heal and we can see that the sutures in the knees are holding, we need to get her up on her feet and moving around, even if the back leg is still painful.' Glen explained the condition in more detail and in such a way that Kirstie could understand. 'You see, the problem here is more in the horse's mind. The injuries in themselves are pretty easy to treat, but she's traumatised.'

Kirstie knelt by Hollywood's head, stroking her neck as usual. She nodded to show that she understood.

'You've heard the expression "turning your face to the wall"?' the vet went on. 'It's like giving up and waiting for death. Well, it looks like that's what's happening here. In other words, if this horse doesn't get back her will to survive, I'm afraid the outlook is pretty poor.'

Sighing and patting Hollywood gently, Kirstie could still hear Lisa's final plea: '*Try as hard as ever you can to get her well again.*'

So she hardly noticed Glen pack his bag and leave, or Ben go away and come back again with a bucket of ice cubes. They clicked and rattled as he plunged his hand in and lifted a fistful out, transferring them into a cotton bag normally used to store curry combs and brushes.

'For her fetlock,' he explained. 'We can't use a hose while she's still lying down, but this should work to cool down the inflammation.'

Picking up a new edge in Ben's voice, Kirstie glanced up. Without his hat, with his shirt collar unbuttoned and sleeves rolled up, he looked younger, the same age as Charlie and Matt. And she noticed a look of concentration in his grey eyes, a determined set to his jaw.

'You think it'll do any good?' she asked, as he placed the bag of ice on Hollywood's back leg.

Ben shrugged. 'What should we do? Wait for her to die?'

'No!' Kirstie felt alarm shoot through her whole body.

'Are we gonna give in and let her turn her face to the wall like Glen said?' He sounded almost angry; no, more like stubborn. That was it: stubborn.

'No way!' Kirstie cried. She offered to hold the ice in place as Ben went for a halter and lead-rope. 'You hear that, Hollywood?' she murmured. 'We're not gonna let you get away with this.'

From her position on the straw bed, Hollywood heaved a great sigh. The sight of the halter in Charlie's hand made her flatten her ears and flick her tail.

'Sure, you might not like it.' Kirstie went on talking gently as the wrangler bent to slip the headcollar on and attach the lead-rope. Her spirits were rising as she felt some of Ben's new determination creep into her. 'And maybe it's gonna take a while until you're feeling your old self again,' she conceded.

Ben was pulling gently on the lead-rope, asking Hollywood to raise her head and think about bending her stiff knees under her.

It was a painful struggle, so Kirstie used her voice to soothe the horse. 'Easy!' she whispered. In her head she said over and over: *You can do it! You can stand!* Then, as Ben used the rope to insist, she spoke more forcefully to the reluctant patient. 'You're a tough ranch horse, remember? A champion cutter. You just have to remember what we do round here when the going gets tough.'

'What's that?' Ben the newcomer asked, coaxing and urging Hollywood to her feet.

The horse's weight was on her injured knees; she was forcing herself to her feet.

Kirstie held her breath, trying not to cry out every time Hollywood gave in and sank to the ground. 'We cowboy up!' she told Ben. 'And, however hard it may be, in the end we make it!'

8

'It's pitiful to see her like this!' Charlie said as he watched Hollywood ease herself slowly to her feet. 'When you think what a great-looking horse she was!'

He went away shaking his head.

'Take no notice!' Kirstie told Hollywood. 'You're on your feet; that's progress!'

It was late Wednesday, only twenty-four hours since Ben and she had first coaxed the horse to stand. Back from school, Kirstie had changed into jeans and a denim shirt and come straight out to pack Hollywood's leg with ice.

Out in the corral she could hear a group of trail-riders returning from their afternoon expedition to Eden Lake. There was the sound of hooves, voices and then footsteps on the wooden porch outside the tack-room.

'Great ride, Ben!' a woman's voice called out appreciatively.

'Yeah, great ride!' a man agreed. 'Hey, Joel, watch what you're doing! You just about took my

leg off riding across the corral like that!'

Joel Martinez was the kid who'd demanded to ride Johnny Mohawk. He was trouble, Kirstie realised. Cocky and careless with both his fellow guests and the horses, he actually seemed to enjoy getting people's backs up. He would swagger into supper and march to the front of the line, grab the biggest helping, then turf another visitor out of his chosen seat at the table. Or else he would barge ahead of others in the queue for tack, wrench Johnny's saddle from the hook and sling it roughly on to the horse's back, despite advice from Ben or Charlie.

The guest from hell, Kirstie thought grimly, examining Hollywood's fetlock and feeling satisfied that the swelling seemed to be less.

'Hey, Kirstie, how's Hollywood doing?' Ben came into the barn as she worked, throwing his hat on to a straw bale and taking off his chaps.

'She's doing great!' Think positive, sound bright and optimistic, she ordered herself.

Ben took in the horse's drooping head and stiff-legged stance. He noticed the still dull and staring

111

coat, the outline of Hollywood's ribcage that showed how much weight had fallen off her since the weekend. 'I got an idea,' he said quietly. 'Wait here.'

'We're not going anywhere, are we, girl?' Kirstie stole Lisa's line as she stood patiently, wondering what the wrangler had in mind.

Joel gave her the first clue. 'What are you doing with my horse?' he demanded from the corral, his voice loud and belligerent.

'This ain't *your* horse,' Ben replied. 'And what I'm doing is taking him visiting, OK?'

She heard the door of the barn open, saw a man and horse outlined against the bright sunlight. Hollywood turned her head and flicked her ears.

'Wait two seconds,' Kirstie called. She grabbed a brush from a nearby ledge, telling Ben that she would let him know when they were ready.

'I gotta fix you up first,' she whispered to Hollywood, starting with the brush across her shoulders. 'A girl can't have visitors until she's looking presentable!'

Swiftly she brushed the dust out of the horse's coat and freed the tangles from her long mane. She pulled the forelock straight and prettified her, ready for Johnny Mohawk to come calling.

'OK!' she called down the aisle of the dim, musty barn.

So Ben walked down with Johnny, who looked curiously this way and that, wondering why he was being brought in here. The black stallion's head was up, ears pricked, until he made out the pale shape of Hollywood Princess standing in her stall in the far corner.

And his presence certainly seemed to have an effect. To Kirstie it was almost like a light switch going on: Hollywood braced herself and raised her head, tilted it to one side and snickered as Johnny came near. She gave him a look, half stand-offish, half flirtatious, then swished her tail and turned disdainfully away.

'Don't be like that!' Kirstie protested with a grin at Ben. This was a great idea to get Hollywood interested in stuff beyond her own injuries. 'Be nice to your visitor! Can't you see that Johnny wants to know how you're getting along?'

The young black horse had come close up to the door of the stall and poked his neck right in. He was nudging Hollywood's shoulder and sniffing at the medication on her wounds, his mouth moving in a chewing motion which said, *Why won't you talk to me?*

Hollywood sighed as if all this sudden attention really was a bore. She turned her head and pushed Johnny away with her nose.

The stallion backed off, looking dejected.

'He won't bother to come again if you act like you don't want him!' Kirstie warned.

Hollywood tossed her head. *Who cares?* Then she had second thoughts. But to get through to Johnny again she must take a couple of steps towards the door. Creakily she lifted one of her stiff front legs and shifted her weight forward. *Clunk!* It hit the stone floor. Her very first step since the accident. The same again, this time with the other front foot, and *clunk!* on to the floor. Hollywood wobbled unsteadily, found her balance and inched towards her admirer.

'Good job!' Ben breathed, watching intently. 'She took some weight on the back fetlock,' he told Kirstie, as the two horses nudged each other affectionately.

And Sandy, who had just come into the stable looking for Kirstie, was in time to see this leap forward in the patient's progress. She nodded and smiled to find Hollywood and Johnny Mohawk together.

'Ben's idea.' Kirstie gave credit where it was due.

'Neat,' Sandy approved.

'What did you want to tell me?' Sidling out of the stall, Kirstie walked the length of the barn with her mom.

'I just had Bonnie on the phone. She told me the latest on Lisa.'

They stopped in the wide doorway, looking out on to the bustling corral. Kirstie shielded her eyes from the low sun and shot Sandy an anxious look.

'Don't worry, things are fine.'

'The hospital still says she can come out soon?'

Sandy nodded. 'Bonnie says all she ever

talks about is Hollywood. "Hollywood and me are gonna do this, and this and this . . . !" It seems she's pinning an awful lot on that horse's recovery.'

'Don't I know it!' Kirstie sighed and felt the good mood over Hollywood's first steps evaporate. After all, it wasn't the rate of progress Lisa would be expecting. And it would be hard for her friend to be patient and logical about this; she would want her favourite horse to be back to normal and nothing less would do. 'When's she due to check out of the hospital?' she asked faintly.

'Bonnie says Saturday morning.'

'That soon?' Kirstie looked over her shoulder at the millions of dust motes dancing in the sun's rays, obscuring Hollywood, Ben and Johnny Mohawk from view.

'Yeah, and I told Bonnie to bring Lisa up to the ranch, just as soon as she thinks she can make it.'

'Which will be Saturday afternoon if I know Lisa.' Just over forty-eight hours away. Kirstie sagged under the weight of the responsibility. Two and a half days to get Hollywood Princess moving around like normal!

'Joel, don't let Johnny drink so much all at once!' Ben yelled at the nightmare guest.

Or, 'Joel, you can get your horse to go where you want without kicking him to bits!' Or, 'Watch out, Joel, no pushing and shoving up the line. And no loping downhill; you know the rules!'

Through Thursday and Friday, everyone on the ranch got tired of hearing the head wrangler trying to pull Joel Martinez into line.

'Don't you just hate that kid?' Kirstie shared her feelings with Hollywood as she walked her steadily up and down the barn.

Right at that moment, Joel was in another stand-off with Ben about taking Johnny out on an extra ride.

'The horse ain't the least bit tired!' Joel protested from the far side of the barn door. 'And what's the problem about me taking him out solo? Hadley let me do that when I was here last fall!'

'Well, I ain't Hadley!'

Kirstie heard Ben's sharp reply and saw the door swing open. She felt Hollywood flinch at the sudden inrush of sunlight. 'Problems?' she asked sympathetically.

Ben flung his hat on the usual stack of straw. 'So what's new? Ever since I took this job, there ain't been nothing but problems!'

Feeling it was wisest not to comment, Kirstie demonstrated instead the new ease with which Hollywood was walking. 'Sure she's still slow,' she admitted, 'but she's definitely improving.'

Ben wanted her to walk the horse back into her stall so that he could check how soon the sutures in her knees could be taken out. 'I asked Glen when I saw him in San Luis earlier today, and he says to leave it to Matt when he gets back from college tomorrow.'

'So it could be this weekend?' Kirstie watched as Ben unwound the layers of tape, bandage and lint. She winced slightly to see the damaged knees: the ragged cuts from the fall still raw and unsightly, the sutures crude and ugly. Then she handed him the tub of ointment that would help reduce the scarring.

'Could be.' Ben was non-committal. He gave a sigh as he stood up straight.

'Hard day?'

'Uh-huh.'

'You want to talk about it?'

'Nope.'

Kirstie frowned at something that had just struck her. 'You know what,' she said, 'you and Hadley are just the same!'

Her comment made Ben turn away sharply. 'No way.'

She followed and stood in his path, leaving Hollywood to nibble at a haynet hanging from the wall. 'Sure you are. You're both the strong, silent type. You never say what you're really thinking.'

'Hmm.'

'You see, that proves my point! "Hmm" is exactly what Hadley would say!'

'Yeah, OK, you got me.' Ben had the grace to half-smile and shrug his shoulders. 'You want to know what's on my mind?'

Kirstie took a guess. 'Joel Martinez?'

'Him and a whole heap of other problems. There's Hollywood for starters.'

'But she's getting better! She's gonna be fine, thanks to all you've done!' She wanted another smile from him, not the worried crease between his eyebrows. Over the last few days she'd been growing fonder of Ben and hated to see the problems getting the better of him.

'Then there's the responsibility of the job,' he confessed. 'I've got the safety of a whole bunch of dude riders on my plate, day in, day out. It ain't easy.'

'Who said it would be?' Kirstie reasoned. 'You knew that when you took the job.'

'Yeah, but—'

'C'mon, that's not the real problem, is it?'

They were digging deep now. Ben had thrust both hands in his pockets and was leaning against a heavy upright post. 'No, you're right. It's not.'

'So what is?'

In the end he gave it to her straight. 'Hadley,' he said. 'That old guy doesn't like me. He reckons

I can't hack it as head wrangler.'

Kirstie stared. 'Hadley? Did he say something?'

'He doesn't have to. The way he looks at me gets right under my skin. And I tell you, I've had it up to here!' Ben raised a hand and made a cut-throat motion. Then he pushed past Kirstie towards the door.

'So what are you gonna do?' she gasped, caught between needing to stay with Hollywood and wanting to follow Ben.

He paused and turned to look over his shoulder. 'I guess I'm gonna quit Half-Moon Ranch,' he said.

'You wanna dance?' Joel Martinez strutted up to Kirstie and planted his cowboy-booted feet square in front of her chair. His dark hair was slicked back with gel, and he moved his permanent wad of gum around his mouth with his tongue.

Friday night was square-dance night, where guests and staff got together for a hoe-down. The dining-room floor had been cleared and a small group of fiddle players and guitarists brought

121

over from San Luis. Everyone got cleaned up and entered into the spirit.

'Do I have to dance with this creep?' Kirstie mouthed at Matt, sitting near the door with his girlfriend, Lachelle. She cringed at the prospect of having her feet trampled and her waist grabbed; if Joel danced like he rode horses, it would be like being caught in a stampede.

'There you go, girl!' A grinning Matt tipped her out of her chair as the music started.

Nightmare! She rolled her eyes at her mom, who was partnering Hadley in the dance. Then she found herself wondering what tactics Lisa would use to cope with the situation. *Dig him in the ribs, kick his shins accidentally on purpose!* Kirstie took the imaginary advice to keep Joel at arm's length, glad when the dance dictated that she switch partners.

'Hey, Hadley!' She sighed with relief as the old wrangler took her hands and guided her through the dance.

'How come you don't look like you're having a good time?' he asked during a linked-arms reel, his eyes narrowed and looking searchingly at her face. 'It ain't that white cutting-horse that's still bothering you, is it?'

'No.' She shook her head and saved her breath for the next long dash down the length of the dance floor. When she met up with Hadley again, she told him that Hollywood was doing very well, thank you.

'That's down to you,' he grunted.

'And Ben,' she added.

'Hmm.' Looking around the room, Hadley saw that the head wrangler was missing out on the hoe-down. He mentioned the fact to Kirstie.

'I guess he doesn't feel like dancing.' Her guard was down, she was hot and breathless as they side-stepped in one big circle around the rim of the floor.

'How come? Is he sick?'

'Not exactly.' She felt Hadley's gaze still fixed on her face.

'What then?' He made it plain that he wanted a straight answer.

So she blurted it out without frills, leaning

sideways to whisper in his ear under the cover of the fiddle music so that no one else would hear. 'Ben's not happy at Half-Moon Ranch,' she confided.

'Not happy?' Hadley echoed, as if the idea was impossible.

'So not happy that he wants to quit!' she hissed. 'And if you must know, Hadley, most of the reason is down to you!'

9

After she'd broken the news to Hadley about Ben
wanting to leave, Kirstie had slipped away from
the dance and run outside to calm herself down.
The cool night and a million bright stars had
drawn her across the yard and out over the
footbridge towards Red Fox Meadow where the
horses grazed.

She could still hear the rapid beat of fiddle
music in the background, still picture the look of

confusion on Hadley's lined, thin face. She wished that words once spoken could be taken back, or that her brain could keep a check on her tongue at times like this.

'Wow, do I wish I hadn't opened my big mouth!' she breathed to Lucky, who had loped the full length of the field to be with her. The palomino's good night vision had allowed him to track her progress all the way from the footbridge, and he was there at the fence before she arrived.

Kirstie climbed on to the top bar and sat astride it. 'What's gonna happen next? What'll Hadley do now that he knows about Ben?'

It was only after she'd murmured these thoughts out loud, that Kirstie realised she wasn't alone at the meadow. There was someone else seeking out the peace and quiet. Finding that he'd been interrupted, he'd set off quickly towards the creek, taking a route that led him away from the ranch house.

Kirstie recognised the tall, slim figure. 'Hey, Ben!' she called after him, her heart in her mouth in case he'd overheard her whispered confidences. She jumped down from the fence and ran to catch him. 'Square dancing isn't your thing, huh?'

'Nope.'

'Me neither.' She slowed down to match his stride, feeling the long grass swish against their legs, smelling the sweet scent of the spring flowers as they brushed by.

There was something in the silence and space of the night that made her blunder on into the very subject she might have been wisest to avoid. *Motor-mouth*, as Matt would have said. 'You're not still thinking of leaving us, are you?'

'Maybe.' Ben strode on, hands in pockets, not looking up.

'But you can't! Who would we get to be head wrangler?'

Silence, except for the swish of feet through grass. 'You could try asking Hadley to take up his old job again,' Ben muttered with a brittle laugh.

Kirstie swallowed hard. 'Listen, Ben, Hadley has never said a single bad word about the way you do your work. Maybe you're reading things into the situation. But you don't want to take it so much to heart. Hadley's Hadley – period!'

'Even so.' He walked on with a shrug.

'And I really rate the way you handle the horses here,' she went on, scrambling over a boulder and splashing into the stream in her effort to keep up. 'You know how a horse *thinks*; you're on their wavelength!'

'Horses ain't the problem. It's the people.'

'Yeah, I know.' This was true. Kirstie frowned and changed tack. 'So, you're gonna give in?'

'Maybe.' Again, the non-committal shrug and refusal to look at her.

So she ran ahead and blocked his way. 'Great!' She raised her voice. 'Yeah, give up, why don't you?'

Ben frowned and turned back to look at the horses in the meadow. Several, including Lucky and Johnny Mohawk, had trotted along the inside of the fence with them. They leaned over the barrier, stretching out their necks and snorting gently.

'Go on, walk away! If what you say is true,

Hadley would love that. He'd have won, wouldn't he? And the Mitzy Donohoes and Joel Martinezes of the world would have beaten you too.' Kirstie paused, amazed at her own daring, frightened that she'd blundered in much too deep. But she was in, so she had to go on. 'Yeah, go ahead; let them win. Quit your job. Why not?'

When she got back to the ranch house, Kirstie had already decided not to mention a word about the conversation she'd had with Ben. She'd left it too much in the air, had run off without waiting for a response, half regretting that she'd pushed him so hard. What was that look on his face as he stood in the starlight taking in what she'd said? Anger? Stubbornness? Defeat? Cave-in?

She couldn't tell, so she'd turned and run.

The square dance was finished and everyone walking up to their cabins, saying goodnight and looking forward to a cosy bed. Sandy, Matt and Lachelle had gathered in the ranch-house kitchen. There was hot chocolate to wind down with after a busy day.

Kirstie took in the scene through the well-lit window as she stepped up on to the porch. Then she started as she saw Hadley in there too, taking her mom to one side and talking quietly with her.

'Oh no!' she gasped and froze. Great! The normally silent Hadley had undergone a personality transplant and opened his big mouth to blab about Ben! Now the whole thing would be blown right open.

Kirstie stayed on the porch as the old man made his way to the door. It swung open and he walked out. Giving him what she hoped was a cold stare, she swept inside.

'. . . No way!' Matt was refusing to believe the news. 'Ben only just started the job. He can't quit already!'

Sandy paced the room, her face drawn. She glanced at Kirstie and saw from her expression that she was up to speed with events. 'How come I'm one of the last to find out?' she complained. 'Hadley knows Ben's plans, so does Kirstie. I'm the one who pays his wages, for heaven's sakes!'

And much as Kirstie protested that Ben hadn't

decided what to do and that Hadley had been wrong to say anything, the damage was done. There was a crisis which had to be dealt with – 'Tomorrow!' Sandy insisted – and another night of guilty conscience stretched ahead for Kirstie as she lay in her bed, tossing and turning.

Saturday dawned cloudy and damp, with a heavy dew. The tops of Eagle's Peak, Hummingbird Rock and Miners' Ridge were shrouded in white mist.

Kirstie was up early, trying to shake off the doom and gloom she felt over Ben, aware that she had lots to do to get Hollywood into shape before Lisa was due to visit the ranch later that day. *Keep busy!* she told herself. *Concentrate on the injured horse.*

So she was out in the barn before breakfast. She strung up a net full of hay, then tempted Hollywood with extra bran and sugar beet, trying to build up some of the weight that had slipped off since the accident.

She mucked out as the horse ate, then got

to work with combs and brushes, planning ahead so that Lisa would be pleased with what she saw.

First off, Hollywood's coat must be groomed into the best possible condition. Her hooves must be picked and oiled, her mane and tail trimmed.

'Hold still!' Kirstie urged, asking Hollywood to take some weight on her sprained fetlock as she lifted the other back foot to pick out the hoof. 'You're gonna have an important visitor, you hear! I've gotta clean you up real good!'

The horse endured the foot-cleaning routine with small shows of impatience. She shuffled around the stall, hiding her head in the corner, refusing to lift her feet to order. But Kirstie persisted, and was already washing Hollywood's mane in tea-tree-oil shampoo when Ben came over from the bunkhouse to see how she was getting along.

'I came to check the sutures,' he said shortly, obviously wanting to avoid the thorny subject of his job, and whether or not he'd mentioned his doubts to Sandy. He went straight into the stall and began to unwind the bandages on Hollywood's knees.

Outside in the corral, Kirstie could hear the start of the day's activities: the sound of hooves and more hustle and bustle as Charlie led horses in from the ramuda. 'I plan to get Hollywood to walk out of the barn into the corral when Lisa arrives,' she told Ben. It would be the first time she'd tried this. 'Do you think she can make it?'

'Maybe.' He inspected the clean wounds and decided to leave the bandages off until Matt had taken a look.

'He said he'd be out here as soon as he'd had breakfast,' Kirstie reported. She hated the awkwardness between them, and the way they were avoiding the big issue. She also felt that if Ben said 'Maybe' one more time and gave that shrug as if to say, 'Don't bug me!', she would scream.

Just like Hadley! she hissed in Hollywood's ear as the wrangler went off to find fresh ointment. *Believe me!*

Hollywood tossed her head and flicked wet

mane into Kirstie's face. *Just get on with the job! Don't tell me your problems, OK!*

It made her laugh. 'OK, I get you. I'm just the beautician around here. I don't have opinions . . . whatever madam says!' She combed the mane and rubbed it dry, made it shine like silk, ready for Lisa's visit.

'Charlie, where's Johnny's saddle?' Joel's voice rose above the general buzz of noise out in the corral.

Hollywood's beauty treatment was over and Matt had come as promised to check the sutures. Ben stood back, arms folded, managing to avoid looking anyone directly in the eye.

'Charlie!' Joel's voice rang out again. 'Where the heck is my horse's tack?'

'You ain't riding Johnny Mohawk today,' Charlie answered. 'Ben wants him to stick around the ranch.'

Kirstie frowned and shot the head wrangler an inquisitive look.

'No way!' Predictably, Joel laid into Charlie. 'I

paid good money to come to this ranch and Johnny is the horse I wanna ride!'

Hearing this, Ben sighed and set off towards the corral. Kirstie followed a few paces behind.

'Hey, Joel!' Out in the daylight, Ben stepped in between Charlie and the argumentative guest. He kept his voice calm as he explained his reasons. 'I need Johnny here for when we bring Hollywood Princess out into the corral for the first time later today. The two horses get on real well. It'll help Hollywood to have him around.'

In the background, Kirstie nodded. Typical good horse sense from Ben.

'Don't give me that!' Joel wasn't having any of it. He wanted to ride Johnny and nothing was going to stop him.

Kirstie watched him turn away from Ben towards the tack-room, determined to find a saddle – any saddle – that he could use.

But the wrangler reached out and held the kid by the shoulder. 'I'm telling you "No",' he said quietly, his grip firm, his gaze unwavering. 'You got that?'

For a second Kirstie thought that Joel was about to give him more lip. But instead he clenched his jaw tight and nodded. 'Got it.'

Ben let him go. 'Fetch Crazy Horse for Joel,' he told Charlie in a firm, calm voice. 'And make sure that Johnny Mohawk stays right where he is.'

'You hear that?' Rushing back to Matt and Hollywood, Kirstie wanted her brother to admit that Ben had handled the situation well.

Matt nodded. 'Wait here. I need my tweezers to take out the sutures.'

He strode off to fetch them, and when he got back, he brought surprise news for Kirstie. 'Your friend just got here,' he told her.

'Lisa?' This was way too early. Kirstie's head went into a spin, thinking of all the things she still had to do, like get Hollywood walking, easing her stiffness, seeing if she could make it the full distance out of the barn.

'Yeah. The hospital discharged her last night. She just drove over with Bonnie. Mom's talking to them right now.'

'But they were supposed to discharge her today, not last night!' This wrecked Kirstie's whole plan. 'The idea is for Hollywood to be looking more like her old self. I promised Lisa!'

'Cool it,' Matt advised, working steadily with the tiny scissors and tweezers to pull out the sutures in the wounds. 'Hollywood's looking as good as you could hope. It's only been a week. Lisa won't be expecting miracles.'

Darting up and down the central aisle, bumping into barrels and boxes, Kirstie hardly listened to Matt's advice. But she did pick up his last words. 'That's where you're wrong,' she insisted. 'Miracles are *exactly* what she's expecting!'

'Then go and tell her they come expensive. She'll have to make do with what we got.'

'You don't understand,' Kirstie muttered. 'I gave my promise!' But there was nothing for it: she would have to go out and say hi to her friend, explain that Hollywood was still an invalid, confined to the barn. Lisa would have to come inside and see the patient in her stall.

No grand entrance for Hollywood; not today at any rate.

Steeling herself, Kirstie went out. She saw Bonnie's car in the yard and Lisa sitting inside. Sandy was leaning through the window, obviously asking her how she was.

'They say she can't take any weight on her hip for at least a couple of weeks,' Bonnie explained as Kirstie approached. 'They gave her crutches.'

'Which I can't use because of my broken collar bone!' Lisa added in an ironic drawl. 'Doh! That's hospitals for you!' She still hadn't seen Kirstie drawing near.

'And she refuses to be pushed around in a wheelchair,' Bonnie was explaining. 'In other words, me and her grandpa have to carry her, and she ain't a lightweight, believe me!'

'Thanks, Mom!' Lisa said huffily. But her face lit up the moment she spotted Kirstie. 'How's that wonderful white horse?' she gabbled impatiently. 'C'mon, bring her into the yard. Let me see her!'

For a split second Kirstie hesitated. Then she knew she didn't have the heart not to try to do what Lisa was asking. 'Wait here . . . yeah, I know, you're not going anywhere!'

She turned and ran back towards the barn. If a miracle was what Lisa wanted, a miracle was what she'd get.

'Easy!' Matt warned.

Ben had rejoined him in Hollywood's stall and together they watched Kirstie fit her headcollar and lead-rope.

'It's OK, we've done this before.' Gingerly she led the horse out of the stall into the aisle. 'We're gonna take it nice and gentle,' she told her. 'And today we're gonna walk just that little bit further, out of that door up ahead, see?'

Hollywood followed, slow and stiff.

'Don't take her through the corral,' Ben advised, his voice taut and edgy. 'It's full of trail-riders and horses getting ready to set off. Lead her out of the side door directly into the yard.'

As usual, Ben's idea was sound. Kirstie decided to take his advice, changing direction, but still having to wait for the stiffness in Hollywood's joints to ease, and especially to make sure that the broken skin across her knees would hold. So their progress towards the lesser used side door was agonisingly slow.

'It's OK, take your time, you're doing great!' Kirstie tried not to let her impatience show. Hollywood had raised her head to take in her surroundings, seemingly listening to the snorts and snickerings of the other horses in the corral.

'Ben!' Kirstie called him softly. 'My guess is she's listening out for Johnny. Can you bring him to meet us?'

The head wrangler overtook them and left by the main door. But his footsteps soon stopped short. 'Charlie . . . where's Charlie? . . . What did he do with Johnny Mohawk?'

Problem! Kirstie kept Hollywood on the move, hoping that Ben would sort it out then use the black stallion to entice Hollywood into the open. 'You're doing good!' she whispered. 'Only a few more steps until we make it to the door.'

The horse was making a big effort, but she was

already tired. Sighing and snorting, she shuffled to a halt.

'OK, we take a break,' Kirstie agreed, listening again to Ben calling for Charlie.

'Over here!' The junior wrangler sounded further off, probably across the other side of the corral, tightening up horses' cinch straps and getting them ready to go.

'I thought I said to leave Johnny tethered nearby!' Ben said.

'That's what I did.' Charlie sounded mystified, then alarmed. 'Hey, who moved him?'

'Where did you leave him?' Ben spoke quickly, urgently.

The case of the disappearing horse! Kirstie shrugged and decided it was time to urge Hollywood through the side door before Lisa got to wondering what was wrong. She felt the horse quiver as she tugged gently at the rope, then gather her energy to do as Kirstie asked.

'You see, we made it!' She pushed the door open and stepped into the yard with Hollywood

. . . and came right up against the missing Johnny Mohawk!

'Go, Johnny!' Joel Martinez was in the saddle, kicking the horse's sides like crazy. 'C'mon, I said go!'

The black stallion stamped and flattened his ears, fighting for his head as his rider tugged hard at the reins.

'Go, man!' Joel yelled, lifting a coil of heavy rope from the saddle horn, letting it snake free and using its knotted end as a whip to lash against Johnny's withers.

'Hey!' Kirstie pulled Hollywood up sharp and yelled a protest. If Joel Martinez thought that he could sneak Johnny round the side of the barn, secretly saddle him up and ride him out on the trail, he'd better think again!

The kid ignored her and laid into his horse with the rope a second time.

Hollywood opened her mouth wide and squealed. Then she tottered forward, reaching out her neck to bite at Joel's leg. He turned the heavy, knotted rope on her, bringing it down against

her shoulder, making Kirstie dive forward to try to catch the end of the rope as it snaked up into the air once more.

And Johnny chose that moment to rear, tossing Joel back in the saddle, snatching the rope out of Kirstie's reach. She was caught off balance, staggering forward, falling to the ground.

Hollywood squealed again. People came running. But Johnny was bucking and kicking in a fury against his rider, who still lashed him savagely.

Kirstie was down, hunched on her side with her knees drawn up to her chest and her hands over her head, feeling the thud of Johnny's hooves inches away, as she lay choking in the dust, crying out for help.

10

Curled up in a ball, Kirstie could hear nothing but hooves thundering down. It seemed to go on for ever: the dust and the shock each time Johnny's front feet landed close to her head.

'Roll to the side!' a voice yelled. It seemed to come from a million miles away, not to make any sense.

She made out a pair of boots in the dirt, screwed her head round to see Ben trying to grab hold of Johnny's flying reins. Joel Martinez was clinging to the saddle horn, his whole body whiplashed back and forth as the horse bucked and reared.

'Roll!' Ben yelled at her again.

This time she understood and did as she was told, gasping and grunting to get clear. She spat grit out of her mouth, got up on to all-fours and began to crawl.

'Kick your legs free of the stirrups!' Ben shot out another command, this time to the desperate rider. 'That's right. Now, let go of the horn, grab hold of my hand!'

She looked up in time to see Joel keel sideways out of the saddle, both hands locked tight around Ben's outstretched arm.

'Jump!' Ben yelled. 'Now!'

In that split second, as the kid launched himself from the saddle and Ben steadied his fall, Johnny Mohawk gave an almighty buck. His back legs exploded and his iron-shod feet crashed against the wall of the barn, splintering the planks. The sound sent him careering across the yard, free of his cruel rider, towards the watching group of Sandy, Bonnie and Lisa.

'Watch out!' Shaken as she was, Kirstie dragged herself to her feet and began to run after Johnny. Lisa's injuries meant she couldn't get out of the path of the spooked horse and Ben was still dealing with Joel. It was up to Kirstie to try and cut Johnny off.

A squeal from Hollywood behind her reminded everyone that the danger wasn't over. Johnny had been sent crazy by the whip; he was trapped in an enclosed space and his instinct was to lash out.

There was too big a gap between herself and the black horse. He was zig-zagging across the yard, lashing his tail, changing course, looking for a way out.

Kirstie was gasping for breath, praying for her mom and the others to get out of the way.

Then Hadley showed up out of nowhere. One minute it was Kirstie trying to cut Johnny off alone, then the old man was there too, standing in the path of the stallion, legs and arms spread wide, eyeball to eyeball with the charging horse.

Johnny saw him and kept on going.

Hadley stood his ground.

He's gonna get himself killed! Kirstie thought.

Instead of sidestepping as Johnny charged, Hadley made as if to take a step towards him. He looked right at him, challenging him, forcing him to veer off course.

Johnny swerved in towards the fence. Hadley followed, arms still stretched wide. He was cornering the runaway, defeating him with sheer willpower.

And it meant Sandy and Bonnie had time to lift Lisa between them and take her out through the gate to safety. It gave Ben the chance to put Joel back on his feet and run to Hadley's aid. Then there was Charlie running into the yard with a lasso, Matt racing out of the barn to join them. Five against one; Johnny felt himself surrounded. He backed into the corner, his head going down in a gesture that said, *OK, you win!*

'Easy, boy!' Still in charge, Hadley moved in closer and closer. 'Nobody's gonna hurt you no more. You stand nice and easy, there's a good boy!'

Johnny stamped and turned restlessly, but he was beaten. His shoulders were flecked with sweat, his sides heaving as he watched and waited.

Holding her place between Matt and Ben, Kirstie watched the old man take hold of Johnny's reins.

'Drama over!' Sandy announced to the audience of trail-riders gathered by the corral fence.

Hadley was leading Johnny quietly away; Joel was sliding off the scene, shamefaced, shaken and bruised.

Kirstie turned back to find out what Hollywood had been up to during Johnny's spectacular revolt, and discovered that the lady was not amused.

Her head was up, ears forward. She'd arched her supple neck and was tossing her silken mane.

In other words, she looked like the horse they'd first met: beautiful-and-don't-I-know-it, sassy, attention-grabbing – however you wanted to describe it, Hollywood was back to her old self.

'Miracle!' Kirstie breathed. What were a couple of scars more or less?

'Wow!' Lisa gasped from the house porch. She had a grandstand view of Hollywood and caught her full glory: the way the thin sunlight made her coat snowy-white, the old look-at-me pose, the perfect proportions of her curved back and small, pretty head.

Set off by the framework of the barn door, the horse drew attention like a magnet. She turned the heads of every single ranch guest, even made Hadley and Johnny Mohawk stop in their tracks before they reached the yard gate.

'Now, don't go tossing your head like that,' Kirstie told her as she walked over quietly and picked up Hollywood's lead-rope. 'These things happen sometimes. No need for you to object.'

But I'm the star around here! The white horse snorted and stamped. She took a few tentative steps forward on her stiff, injured legs, then overcame the discomfort. She strode out more smoothly, glancing this way and that to make sure that all eyes were on her.

'Yeah, yeah!' Kirstie managed to hide the thrill she felt as Hollywood strutted her stuff. After all, there was no need to make her more big-headed than she already was. 'Come and see Lisa,' she coaxed. 'She's been real worried about you.'

Hollywood walked on, easier and more flowing, lifting her legs in a prancing step, shimmying past Johnny Mohawk, whose gaze was fixed on her every move.

And with the help of Sandy and Bonnie, Lisa came down from the porch, up to the fence. She was there when Hollywood and Kirstie arrived, ready to stroke the smooth white neck.

'What can I say?' she whispered, her voice choked as she stared into Hollywood's big eyes.

Looking very closely over Lisa's shoulder, Kirstie caught her friend's reflection in the horse's dark brown eyes. She could see that though the words wouldn't come, the tears did.

'Hey,' she murmured. 'What's with the crying?

Didn't I tell you Hollywood would make it?'

Lisa wiped her eyes and stuck out her chin. As if there had ever been a moment's doubt!

A dude ranch in the Rockies. A camp fire under the stars. Cue music.

Kirstie sat next to Lisa, their faces aglow from the yellow, crackling flames. Tonight the Saturday cook-out seemed special, and not only because Matt had been persuaded to bring along his guitar.

'You OK?' Kirstie checked that Lisa was comfortable on the blanket she'd spread on the grass next to the creek.

'Yeah. Quit fussing around!' Lisa made it clear that just because she'd spent a week in hospital, she wasn't like fine china and about to break into small pieces. She'd spent the day at Half-Moon Ranch trying to prove that, like Hollywood Princess, she was made of sterner stuff. And now there was music and singing, and she wanted to forget the accident. 'So, what's new?' she asked.

'Joel Martinez left for Denver this afternoon,' Kirstie reported with undisguised satisfaction. 'Matt reckons this will have been his last visit to the ranch.'

'Good.' Lisa pulled her jacket round her shoulders; the collar snagging on her neck-brace made her wince as she moved closer to the fire. 'What else?'

'We have a biology test Monday.'

'Boring!'

Kirstie grinned. She looked round at Matt

playing guitar, surrounded by a small group of people humming or singing along. 'OK, get this: Ben might quit his job!'

The incident with Johnny Mohawk had taken it clean out of her mind until this moment, but now she spotted the wrangler sitting apart from the others, like he didn't belong. He'd chosen a spot out of the firelight, down on the footbridge, letting his long legs dangle only inches above the water as he stared into the fast-flowing current.

'Gee, why?' Lisa wanted to know every detail, and kept up a string of questions as the music grew louder.

'. . . So, Hadley really messed up by telling Mom, because I was doing my best to get Ben to stay. But now Mom knows, and the pressure is on for him to make a decision, 'cos she says she wants it sorted by the end of today, and look at Ben now, sitting over there and all—'

'Kirstie!' Lisa cut in to warn her that Ben had stood up and was wandering towards the campfire.

By coincidence, so was old Hadley Crane, who

had come out of the barn to join the crowd. He made a bee-line for Matt, pulled a silver mouth-organ out of his top pocket and began to play the tune.

'Did Ben see him yet?' Kirstie whispered.

'I guess not!' Lisa could see that the young wrangler was still making his way towards the fire. 'Look, he wants to talk with your mom!'

'Oh no!' This could only mean one thing: Ben was seeking Sandy out to tell her his decision. And Kirstie couldn't read his expression in the flickering light.

She and Lisa followed his actions closely as he skirted the crowd and made his way to the opposite side of the fire. He crouched down between Bonnie and Sandy, hands clasped in front of him.

'Will your mom beg him to stay?' Lisa hissed.

Kirstie shook her head. 'Not if he's got it in his head that he has to quit.'

Sandy listened without reacting, except to nod every now and then.

Lisa and Kirstie craned to see better, holding their breath as Ben stood up and took a few steps back out of the light.

That's it, then! Kirstie thought. *He quit!*

She hardly noticed that the music had stopped for Matt to re-tune his guitar. But then she saw Hadley slip from his place and thread his way towards the spot where they'd last seen Ben. 'Wait here!' she whispered to Lisa, who pointed to her neck-brace and to her painful hip. 'Yeah, OK, sorry!'

So she went by herself, picking out the two dark figures of Hadley and Ben walking together across the footbridge towards the ramuda. Was it a good sign that they were talking, or bad? Should she catch them up or bite back her curiosity and leave them alone?

No, she needed to know. So she picked up speed as they approached the meadow.

'. . . You reckon Hollywood's knees will heal well enough for her to get back to work?' Ben was asking Hadley's advice.

Good sign! Kirstie told herself. *But then again, maybe not.*

'Not for ranch work.' Hadley told it like it was.

'That kind of injury would mean the end for a cutter or a roper. But for a trail-riding horse, it should be OK.'

'Hmm.' Ben nodded and walked on.

'Hollywood's a nice horse,' Hadley conceded.

Good sign! This time Kirstie felt more certain; Hadley was doing his best to make up with Ben.

'Yup.'

'I never saw a better American Albino in forty years.' Hadley kept pace with the young wrangler, while Kirstie followed behind, hoping to eavesdrop invisibly. They'd reached the fence of Red Fox Meadow and easily picked out Hollywood Princess from the rest of the horses. Ben had put her out to graze for the first time since the accident, fencing her into a corner with electric wire to protect her from the hurly-burly of the herd.

The two men said nothing for a while as Hollywood came slowly through the grass in peaceful, gentle mood. She made for Ben and nuzzled him softly, getting the strokes and affection she knew she deserved.

'Put it there, partner!' Ben murmured, holding out the palm of his hand.

Hollywood lifted her foot and shook hands.

Brilliant! Kirstie's heart swelled, but still she didn't step forward.

There was another long, unbroken period when nothing was said and nothing could be heard except the restful tearing and chewing of grass.

Then Hadley broke the silence. 'So you quit?' he asked gruffly, eyes on the white horse, voice giving nothing away.

It seemed to Kirstie that Ben's answer took ages, aeons; she held her breath and looked up at the stars.

'Nope,' he muttered at last, looking over his shoulder at Kirstie with a small grin, just between the two of them.

He knew she'd been there all along, and he enjoyed having her there as an audience as he delivered his final decision to his old rival. 'I got a lot of work to do: horses to look out for, riders to keep in line. And I only just started, so I guess I'm gonna be around for a little while yet!'